AWAY WE GO

EMIL OSTROVSKI

GREENWILLOW BOOKS, AN IMPRINT OF HARPERCOLLINS PUBLISHERS

Away We Go

Copyright © 2016 by Emil Ostrovski

All rights reserved. No part of this book may be used or reproduced in any manner whatsoever without written permission except in the case of brief quotations embodied in critical articles and reviews. Printed in the United States of America. For information address HarperCollins Children's Books, a division of HarperCollins Publishers, 195 Broadway, New York, NY 10007.

www.epicreads.com

The text of this book is set in 11-point Chaparral Pro.

Book design by Steven Scott

Library of Congress Cataloging-in-Publication Data is available.

ISBN 978-0-06-223855-9 (hardback)

16 17 18 19 20 CG/RRDH 10 9 8 7 6 5 4 3 2 1

First Edition

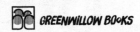 GREENWILLOW BOOKS

**To my parents, who let me spend
my summers writing**

PROTECT YOUR CHILDREN
THE TRUTH ABOUT PPV

WHAT IS IT?

▶ PPV (Peter Pan Virus) is an infectious, airborne disease that affects children and young adults. It is nearly always fatal.

HOW MANY CHILDREN ARE INFECTED?

▶ The CDC estimates that there are as many as two hundred thousand youths in recovery in the United States alone, with up to twenty thousand new cases reported each year.

▶ Since its discovery, PPV has claimed twenty-three million lives worldwide.

WHEN DOES INFECTION OCCUR?

▶ Infection typically occurs prior to the onset of puberty, though individuals as old as seventeen have become infected. The average age at diagnosis is eight.

WHAT ARE THE SYMPTOMS OF PPV?

▶ Immediately upon infection, the infected child will experience coldlike symptoms for up to two weeks.

▶ The secondary stage of PPV can last anywhere from three to ten years, with treatment. Symptoms are manageable, and may include but are not limited to coughing, sore throat, prolonged stiffness or numbness, muscle and joint pain, impaired respiratory function, and impaired vision or hearing. In rare cases, intermittent loss of consciousness can occur. Placement is usually in a recovery center.

▶ The tertiary stage is characterized by the onset of symptoms such as memory loss, hallucinations, loss of motor control, seizures, paralysis, coma, organ failure, and death. Placement is usually in a specialized tertiary care clinic or other hospice facility.

HOW CAN I KEEP MY CHILD SAFE FROM PPV?

▶ Quarterly checkups are mandatory! Early diagnosis and quarantine of infected youths is essential to keeping your children safe!

MY CHILD HAS PPV. WHAT ARE THE TREATMENT OPTIONS?

▶ Recovery centers and recovery clinics are staffed by the nation's leading medical care professionals. These doctors and researchers will work to create a specialized treatment regimen for your child.

▶ Early diagnosis and proper medical treatment are essential to improving an infected youth's prognosis.

MY CHILD IS IN RECOVERY. WHY CAN'T I VISIT THE TREATMENT CENTER? WHY ARE OUR COMMUNICATONS MONITORED?

▶ The primary goal of the National Recovery Program is to provide for general safety and well-being. In light of past incidents, it has become necessary to institute certain policy changes. These include the suspension of visitation rights and the surveillance of all incoming and outgoing communications. To facilitate this process, all incoming and outgoing communications must be in the form of regular mail.

MY CHILD IS IN RECOVERY. HOW CAN I FACILITATE HIS OR HER ADJUSTMENT TO RECOVERY CENTER LIFE?

▶ Studies show that regular correspondence with an infected youth reduces the emotional trauma of separation and eases the transition to life in a recovery center. If you would like to correspond with your child, please send a letter to the National Recovery Program's mail processing center at 1700 Pennsylvania Ave. NW, Washington, D.C. 20006-4700, making sure to print your child's recovery ID next to his or her name. Mail will be processed in a timely fashion, in accordance with the order in which it is received.

A YEAR AND A
HALF BEFORE THE
CATACLYSMIC,
FIERY, KIND OF
CLICHÉD END
OF ALL THINGS
(OR NOT)

AWAY TO WESTING

I was fifteen years old.

It was a dreary March day, a year and a half before the world was supposed to end. And the closest person I had to family wanted me gone.

Alex and I spent most of our time in a converted bathroom that the administration of the Richmond Youth Recovery Center for Boys had stuffed with books and called a "library." Nobody cared enough to dispute the title. The library's reading selection ranged from *The Little Engine That Could* to *On the Fourfold Root of the Principle of Sufficient Reason*, and while the stalls and the sinks had been ripped out to make way for bookshelves, a lone urinal had inexplicably been left standing against the far wall, so half the library's visitors were boys whose interest in relieving their overfull bladders far exceeded that of engaging with the world republic of letters. We were settled in a corner of the library, passing a cig between us. Footsteps pattered down the hallway. Alex brushed a lock of brown hair away from his eyes, handed the cig to me, and asked me what I thought about Director Mary's latest spiel.

I sucked in the smoke, held it in my throat as long as I could.

"*Noah*," he said. "You even listening or those ears just for show?"

"Huh?" I croaked.

I had been studying his perpetually dirty nails.

"You know, No," he said. "What Mary Poppins said about taking the NAAPs and getting the *fuck* out of here, son."

"You mean you were actually at assembly?" I said in mock disbelief.

Alex took offense. "Fuck no, No," he said. "But word gets around."

I shrugged. "Well, *Al*. Even if we take the NAAPS, and honestly I'd rather take a nap instead—"

"Oh God," he said, feigning an allergic reaction to my punniness, gasping for breath.

I nudged him with my shoulder gently. "And even if we take the NAAPs, and get like perfect scores, the chances of getting into Westing are *minute*."

"Look at you. Using words like 'minute,'" Alex said. "You definitely don't belong here."

"There's no point, man," I said. "We're going away in a few years max, no matter if we're at Westing or Richmond."

"Richmond's library"—Alex pointed to the far wall—"has almost as many urinals as books. I hear Westing is like a fucking castle. Gothic architecture and shit. And stained-glass windows, son."

"The chances are *minute*." I wanted to tell him his nails were disgusting. I wanted to kiss him.

"I'll NAAP if you will," I finally offered, and waited for him to take me up on it.

When he met my eye, it was with a pitying look, the kind that says: *Have you always been slower than a tertiary-stage relay team, or is this a new development?*

"It would be pointless for me," Alex said. "There are kids who've never shown up to class who have higher GPAs."

"Maybe if you do really well on the NAAPs—"

"Please, son," Alex said, rolling his eyes. He didn't say it, but he meant: *Grow up*.

"Then I'm not applying. Or taking the test."

"I'd do it if I were you."

I opened my mouth to ask him if he meant that, if he'd really leave me behind, but I stopped myself.

I didn't want to know.

There was no more talk about the NAAPs. I didn't study or take the prep classes. But a few weeks later, on a muggy Saturday in mid-April, Alex shook me awake at nine a.m., pulled me half naked out of my bunk bed, and made me dress myself.

I was in a semi-comatose state and thus did not muster much of a protest. Eventually, I caught a glimpse of the time on our wall clock and asked desperately, "What's going on?" I hadn't gotten up at nine a.m. on a Saturday since before my balls dropped. Usually I skipped breakfasts on the weekends (if the weekdays were anything to go by, I wasn't missing much) and went straight from bed to lunch.

Alex didn't answer. He was bent over, rummaging through my footlocker. He tossed a pair of socks over his shoulder, not looking. They hit me in the face.

"What the fuck," I said.

A pair of jeans followed.

"What the fuck."

He turned, saw the jeans and socks on the floor. "Hurry up," he said.

"What—"

"Trust me, son."

"But—"

"Don't be a bitch."

After I dressed myself, he grabbed me by the arm and led me through our dormitory, crammed with the bodies of over two hundred snoring boys, down a number of gray and peeling hallways, and into our gym. He practically threw me into one of the few remaining chairs.

"Sit," he ordered.

Before I could say a word, he told me, "Stay." He exchanged a few words with the proctor at the front of the class. I counted maybe twenty other boys who'd come to take the test. He returned with "a present." He deposited this present, which looked suspiciously like an NAAP, on my desk. Frowned at me. Said, "Oh yeah." Thrust his hand in his pocket, took out a dull pencil, and placed it next to the test packet masquerading as a present.

I waited for him to change his mind. Maybe he'd sit down to take the test with me. But instead he gave me a two-finger salute, turned on his heel, and left.

A couple weeks after that Saturday on which so many hours of sleep were stolen from me, the teachers posted our scores on the gym wall.

I got a 150. Better than anyone else at Richmond. Still, it wasn't good enough, not for a place like Westing, the only recovery center of its kind in the entire National Recovery Program. Supposedly a prototype for the next generation of recovery centers, for now it was where America herded away its best and brightest to recite Eugene Onegin, live in progressive coed dorms that challenge the gender binary, and, eventually, disappear like all the other infected kids. The official story was that kids too sick for regular recovery centers got transferred to tertiary care clinics, but Alex maintained the government probably shipped us off to Area 51 to be dissected by aliens—a popular theory.

I stumbled through the cafeteria crowds, everyone soaked in sweat, because the AC wasn't working again. I wanted to tell Alex the good news: *I'm staying, bitch.* His chosen table had a crack down the middle and graffiti of the *Suck my dick* variety covering every bit of the surface. He was picking at one of the slightly green gelatinous globs that passed for mac and cheese at Richmond. A small plastic bag lay next to his plate.

"Yummy," I said as I sat down across from him.

"If you say so," he said, biting absentmindedly at a dirty nail.

"What's in the bag?"

He reached in to produce a chocolate bar. Wiggled it. He must've bought it from one of the dealers; probably paid a fortune for it, too. Anything from outside cost a fortune. He slid it over to me.

"Your congratulatory feast."

"What do you mean?"

"Come on, son. Don't ruin it."

"I didn't get a one sixty. Not even close."

"You beat the next closest guy by five points," he said. "If anyone gets in from here, it'll be you."

"I'm telling you it's not good enough." I'd felt relief when I saw my score. I could barely remember my parents, my brother, so their loss was like the loss of a dream you forget upon waking. But Alex was as solid as the ground beneath my feet. "I'm not applying."

"Yeah, you are."

"What is wrong with you?" I said, my frustration finally spilling out.

"What is wrong with *you*?" He was angrier than I'd ever seen him.

"Westing can suck it," I replied, inspired by the graffiti.

Alex closed his eyes. He spoke in a tone of forced evenness. I had to lean in to hear.

"Oh, No. My bro." He opened his eyes and flashed me a thin smile. "It'll be good for you there. Trust me. If you don't want to do it for yourself, do it for me."

"And besides," he continued, "at Westing you'll be able to get some pussy." He said this with a decisive air, as if he felt that should settle the matter once and for all. But I didn't *want* pussy. Without access to girls, guys at Richmond sometimes took to experimenting with each other. What Alex and I had done, I'd liked.

"And Noah?"

"Yeah?" I was using my sulky voice.

"For your essay?"

"Yeah?"

"Write it on your acting."

I pictured the Westing admissions committee, a group of old prunes I'd never met sitting in suits at a glass conference table, all quiet and regal and trying not to pass gas, weighing the decision of whether to admit Jacob S. or Sarah P. with such gravitas you'd have thought the papers in their lined, neatly manicured hands contained an imprint of the applicants' souls.

Instead of writing the essay to them, I wrote it to Alex. In reading my essay to Alex, the admissions committee read of me performing plays real and imagined in closets and bathrooms, and on the roof of Richmond at half past two on many a winter morning. "'To be or not to be?'" I once asked the dark and snowy sky. I hadn't merely said the words. I'd stood at the edge of the roof and meant them.

In late July, a few weeks short of my sixteenth birthday, I heard back.

Dear Mr. Noah Falls,

We are pleased to extend to you an offer of admission to Westing Academy as a junior for the fall of the upcoming school year. We reviewed thousands of applications for admission, many submitted by very qualified and talented young individuals from a variety of unique and diverse backgrounds. Unfortunately, offers of admission could be made only to a select few of these applicants. You have been chosen for your extraordinary academic and extracurricular achievements, which reveal you to be a dedicated young person capable of representing the Academy well. As one of the only institutions of our kind in the world, and the only such institution in the United States, we take pride in our mission here at Westing, a mission that can only be carried out through the continued success and diligence of our pupils. We hope you will be joining us this fall as a student, as a representative, and as a soldier willing to do his part in the battle for improved conditions for all youths in recovery. Once again, congratulations.

Sincerely,

Adam B. Colters

Adam B. Colters
Dean of Admissions
Westing Academy

We spent my last night at Richmond on the roof, looking out at the fields beyond Richmond's walls. It was a brisk night in early September, one of the first autumn nights, and what I wouldn't have given for a five-minute run through the surrounding countryside, a chance to dash headlong into that wind. Just thinking about it made me dizzy with excitement—I could hardly remember a time I wasn't surrounded by walls. I said so to Alex.

"I mean, sure, I'd probably trip and fall on my face, but up to that point it would be sweet."

He didn't respond at first. "I wonder why they don't round us all up and shoot us. Instead of sticking us in centers. Burn the bodies. Stop PPV from spreading once and for all. That would be best."

When I didn't answer, he added, "Better than being some alien lab experiment."

"If I was an alien and you were my lab experiment, I would send a probe to Uranus."

"Stop," he said, pretending to be annoyed, but he couldn't keep from laughing.

At Richmond, we had little connection with the outside—no Internet, no cable, a bin of old movies to watch on a TV more ancient than our parents. But we could see that despite our being "in recovery," more kids kept showing up at Richmond, red-eyed and fresh from their diagnoses. These fresh faces brought news of the government's billion-dollar National Recovery Program, recovery centers like Richmond cropping up all over the country. There were whispers of medication shortages and internment camps—sorry, improvised mass recovery clinics—at the same time that the government was reportedly spending hundreds of millions of dollars on Westing. A kid named Jeremy Bertram claimed his dad was a tertiary care researcher who had pioneered a medical procedure that had cured several infected kids of PPV, whereas Jason Waters maintained tertiary care clinics were slaughterhouses in which infected kids rolled down an assembly line until a man in a rubber suit shot them in the forehead. Sanjeev Kapoor told us about how in Mumbai, parents wouldn't let children outside—those who had money sent their kids into the country, away from the cities. A devout Catholic boy appropriately named Christian wouldn't shut up about an attempt on Pope John Paul III's life; despite the fact that the gates of heaven were cracked wide for His Holiness, Pope John Paul apparently proved remarkably resilient to assassination, because the would-be assassin—Marco Rinaldi—had the distinction of being the only man in history to have been head-butted repeatedly in the face by Christ's acting representative on Earth.

Alex studied my face, my silence. "You know I'm right."

"I think I'll pass," I said. I didn't want him to be right. "You said you missed your parents' lake house."

"More than my parents. Mom was always working and Dad was always mad that Mom was always working."

"But you remember them?" I could hardly remember mine. We weren't allowed direct contact with them, in light of past incidents, which was government speak for kidnappings, runaway attempts, highway chases, terrorist attacks, contamination alerts. Seven years ago, a few months before I got sick, the entire city of Houston was put under quarantine after a handful of armed and desperate Texan parents raided the South Houston Boys' Recovery Center. A hundred infected youths escaped into the general population; the mayor of Houston declared a state of emergency, and Governor Johnson called up the National Guard.

From beside me, a snort. "Yeah, whoop-dee-doo." But I could tell he didn't mean it. He rubbed at his eye angrily with a knuckle.

"Pinkeye?"

"Shut up," he said, and kicked me lightly in the shin.

"Hey," I said after a time, to break the silence that had settled over us. "Can I ask you for something weird?"

He pitched his head forward in a nod and listened to my request, and said "Oh, No," in agreement, in the softest voice I'd ever heard him use. In the recovery center's second floor bathroom, across from the dormitory, he let me wash his hands with warm water and soap. They were coarse. I worked intently, finger by finger, until his nails were clean.

SEVEN WEEKS
BEFORE THE
CATACLYSMIC,
FIERY, KIND OF
CLICHÉD END
OF ALL THINGS
(OR NOT)

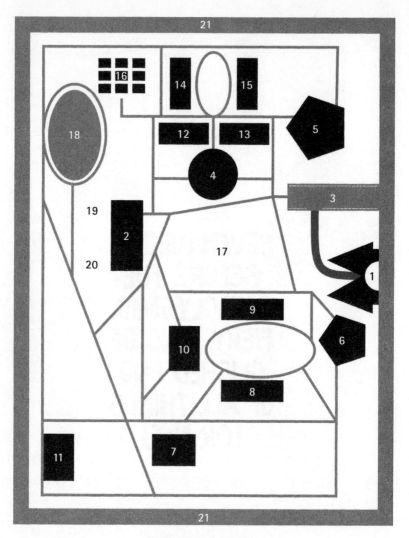

WESTING CAMPUS

1 - Main Gate
2 - Galloway Hall
3 - Teacher's Lot
4 - Wellness Center
5 - Chapel
6 - Library
7 - Cafeteria

8 - Bullsworth Hall
9 - Gates Hall
10 - Lombardy Hall
11 - Greenhouse
12 - Dorlan House
13 - Violet House
14 - Clover House

15 - Turner House
16 - Lakeside Apartments
17 - Galloway Lawn
18 - Westing Lake
19 - Sunset Hill
20 - Galloway Gardens
21 - The Westing Wall

THE REASON I STICK AROUND

Atoms are mostly empty space.

I am mostly empty space.

I have been thinking about this a lot.

I am thinking about this as I step into the shallows of the Westing Lake, the apartments on the far shore white and blinding in the August sun. Beyond the Lakeside Apartments are the walls that enclose the Westing campus.

I do not remember a time when I wasn't surrounded by walls.

The water is surprisingly cool. Another step and it will be up to my balls. I may be empty, but I am not ready for that shock just yet. I leave my clothes on so, if worst comes to worst, I can comfort myself with the thought that my modesty won't be compromised as I sink to the bottom of the lake.

I've been thinking a lot about Alex. He was older, must've wanted me gone before he got bad. I'm a week short of seventeen now, running on borrowed time myself. I've sat for hours on the Internet, searching for Alex in a place I know I won't find him, AwayWeGo's DEPARTEES section. Got to hand it to whoever came up with the idea of a social network for the terminally ill. The site's in its trial stages now, restricted to Westing students, but they're going to make a killing on us—ha—when in a few years it gets rolled out to recovery centers across the whole country.

That is, if we're still here in a few years.

If Apep, the mile-long asteroid I refer to as the Great Cliché, passes us by.

Maybe at that point, if we're still here, and if someone cares, someone who is decent, they will take the time to revise the names that fill the DEPARTEES pages, and add Alex to the list. By then I'll probably be a departee myself.

I rush forward into the water.

But maybe—*stroke*—before that happens—*stroke*—I'll find out where it is that the sick kids go, and why we never hear from them again.

For now, I swim, even though I'm supposed to be staying out of the sun. The side effects of the meds we choke down at our weekly checkups are different for everyone. For me, the meds dry my skin out, make it peel. Sometimes it bleeds.

I call it my minor case of leprosy.

The sky is unflaggingly blue, the light of day hiding a thousand thousand stars, and another thousand thousand beyond those—stars I'll never see even in the night. Something to do with dust and the acceleration of the universe, with galaxies hurtling ever more quickly away, away, always away. Or so the scientists say. Once they told us the galaxies would fly together, dragged by gravity to relight a primordial fire, on and on and on again. Now the galaxies are fleeing.

Somewhere up there, too, is The Great Cliché, with its one-in-ten-thousand chance of hitting the Earth this September twenty-sixth at 11:37 p.m.

It is the ultimate proof that life is a joke, as empty and fleeting as a walking shadow.

Out, out, brief candle!

All human civilization, the Pyramids of Giza, the *Bhagavad*

Gita, the Noble Eightfold Path, Beethoven's *Moonlight Sonata*, Groucho Marx's pithy grouchiness, cheese fries, all of it so fragile as to be reduced to nothing by a really big rock sling-shotting randomly through space. An end so banal it's featured in at least a dozen AwayWeWatch movies starring large-muscled men who shout, "Get it together, man!" at their panicked teammates during times of high apocalyptic stress.

Yes, the world is full of clichés.

Pandemics, killer comets.

All that's missing is a zombie or two.

Before we add zombies to our end-of-the-world recipe, though, I must visit the most confusing person in the world.

His name is Zach, and he is the main reason I stick around.

POSSIBLY THE MOST CONFUSING PERSON IN THE WORLD

Possibly the most confusing person in the world is lying in bed with his laptop on his lap top, listening to an audiobook through AwayWeRead. He grins weakly upon seeing my face. He's pale and sweaty, sometimes has difficulty catching his breath. We end up talking about vegetables while an adolescent narrator named Winston describes in a haunted tone a seemingly utopian city called City, the last bastion of human civilization on a ruined earth.

"Today's a good day," Zach says, playing with his shirt collar. He's the only guy I know who doesn't look like an asshole with the top couple buttons undone. "I ate a baby heirloom tomato. Managed to hold it down, too."

"A baby tomato," I repeat.

"A baby heirloom tomato, kid, just popped it in my mouth. Someone had them in the fridge down in the multipurpose room—"

"You stole someone else's baby tomato?"

"Baby heirloom tomato," he says, nodding vigorously. "I know, I know, I *know*. I'm a monster."

"You always were a bad role model."

"The worst!" he exclaims in triumph. "I'm a madman."

"Lovecraft called. He wants his Mountains of Madness back."

He laughs, and his laugh pokes a small hole in my heart, as does each line of banter, each repartee. He is trying heroically to pretend things aren't awkward between us, and I am trying heroically not to make things more awkward by asking him why they have to be awkward in the first place, when his presence gives me, I don't know, such an ease of being. He makes the emptiness lift, briefly, makes me feel—*tangible*.

It doesn't hurt that, even sickly and soon to depart, he is beautiful in the morning light. He pushes himself up a bit and presses a key on his laptop to pause the audiobook's narration, leans back against his headrest with a sigh.

I want to say something memorable, to do something other than make him laugh. I want to make him feel something more dangerous than amusement.

"What were you listening to?" is what I ask instead, even though I already know. Dystopians are the latest craze on AwayWeRead. Everyone at Westing, myself included, reads every dystopian they can get their hands on and then talks shit about anyone who reads every dystopian they can get their hands on, since what we're supposed to be doing is paging through Thomas Mann's *Buddenbrooks* or Henry James's *The Turn of the Screw*. But who is to say that some stories are better than others? When your time is limited, who is to say you should spend seven hundred pages trodding through the decline of an infuriatingly mediocre family of German merchants when Winston's adventures are so much more fun, and better paced? And if there is no such authority who decides which stories are better and which worse, then does that mean all stories are equal? And if all stories are equal, what does it mean to live a good life? Is there such a thing? And if there isn't, then you start to feel like a whole lot of nothing, again. . . .

"You'll make fun of me," he says with a smile. "God, you'll make fun of me. Promise me you won't?"

"I make no guarantees."

He laughs again, and there goes the pain in my chest.

"*The City of Light*," he says, and eyes me with expectation, waiting for me to crack. He adds, "You can't tell anyone. Especially not our fellow Polo aficionados. What would they say about their glorious leader?"

"I made no guarantees," I remind him.

"We've established I'm a monster, though, kid. Do you want to mess with a monster?"

"Do your worst."

"Don't make me eat another baby heirloom tomato, Noah."

"Say baby heirloom tomato. One. More. Time. Zach."

Before he can say what I know he wants to say one more time, my phone buzzes. I ignore it, but he nods at my pocket.

"Could be important."

"Sometimes," I say, hesitating. Dangerous. I need to say something dangerous. "Sometimes, when my phone rings, I think for a second it might be my parents."

It's crazy to even mention getting a call from outside Westing. It's not like I even want to talk to my parents, not like I even know who they are, anymore. And yet. . .

"Is that crazy?" I ask.

He's fingering his collar. "No," he says softly. "Or rather, crazy normal, I think."

I don't quite know how to respond, so I check my phone.

where are you??

are you sleeping again??

how much sleep do you need??

i never see you doing work??

All from my old roommate and current best friend Marty,

whom I was supposed to meet for a late breakfast.

I glance at the time and suppress a groan. People were never late until time was invented to tell them otherwise.

"Shit," I say, and throw Zach an apologetic look, but a part of me is relieved.

Zach and I are most manageable to each other in small doses.

I'm at his door when he calls me back.

"Wait."

He reaches into his nightstand, breathing hard. His hand shakes a little as he takes something out.

"Come here."

He watches me with a bemused expression as I approach him warily.

"Hold out your hand."

I hesitate. "Are you going to give me a baby heirloom tomato?"

He laughs, but the laugh turns into a grimace.

I've caused him pain. So I try to make up for it. I hold out my hand.

He drops a key into it.

Polo Club's key.

The one we stole.

My hand closes around it.

"You'll be the keeper of the key from now on. A most esteemed position within the ranks of our noble order. My way of saying sorry."

I don't know why he's giving it to me.

I don't know what it means that he's giving it to me.

I want things to be simple.

I want an ease of being, because when it's easy to be alive, it feels like you're doing something right. It feels like you're adding up to something.

I want to lean in and brush his sweat-slick hair out of his eyes, fall into bed together, share his sickness, his fatigue, listen to sixteen-year-old Winston in *The City of Light* discover that his utopian city runs on the backs of thousands of slaves who are born, work, and die in underground factories without ever once stepping foot into the light.

Yes, I've read it.

Yes, in one sitting.

Yes, till three a.m.

That's not the point.

The point is I want him to banter into my chest and to be unable to make his words out, but laugh anyway, out of certainty that if I had heard, it would've been funny, and also, of course, because his breath would tickle.

Instead, I thank him, and leave him to his city of light.

THE NEXT BEST THING

Breakfast meant something to me in the days before Westing or Richmond, days of blurred faces and muted words. I would make my way down the stairs of our house on Sunday morning to the smell of syrup and butter. Grandma and Grandpa used to cook breakfast for us on Sundays. Grandma liked to chase Grandpa around the kitchen with a wooden spatula.

They must be dead by now.

There's a path I love that starts at the lake, arcs behind Galloway, and ends at the rear of the cafeteria. On a whim, I drop by the campus store in Galloway to buy Marty a present to say I'm sorry for always being late, something silly, and then I'm running for the cafeteria, the cobblestones under my feet wet from the morning drizzle. They look like glass. If not for the shade from the evergreens, I might catch my reflection in them. For no reason at all, I close my eyes. Sometimes I do this. Walk with my eyes closed. The sound of an engine interrupts my Zen. I open my eyes, step off the path. A Westing security officer whizzes by in a cart. The Believers are waiting on the cafeteria steps, holding their *The End Time Is Your Time* signs. A pretty boy with unruly hair flashes a smile at me, and while I'm momentarily taken off guard, shoves a flyer in my face.

In the cafeteria, I crumple the flyer and decide I'm not hungry, in spite of my stomach's grumbling protests to the contrary. I find Marty at a table off to the side, hunched into himself, as if to minimize the space he takes up in the world. Of course, he doesn't notice me. He's bent over a copy of *War and Peace*, scratching absentmindedly at the dark caramel skin of his forehead.

I clear my throat.

He looks up from the book and says, "Oh," by which he means, "You're here."

I offer him his present—the Westing basketball cap I bought at the campus store—as a "token of our undying friendship." An inside joke, seeing as how we're both such tremendous sports buffs, he and I. Drinking five shots of vodka is an act of great endurance, right?

He laughs.

"It's a bit sweaty," I say, "but what's a little exchange of bodily fluids between friends?"

He dons the cap frontward, which is ridiculous. I reach over, adjusting it so that it's backward.

"There," I say.

"I feel so cool," he says.

I'm so happy I want to hug Marty. He reminds me that things don't have to be complicated.

"I disapprove of your life choices," I say, indicating the sandwich on his plate.

He gives me a cheeky grin. "You've made your feelings about sandwiches clear before."

"That they're culinary atrocities?"

"Uh-huh." He takes a bite.

"That those who eat them are heretics?"

"Urh-hurh," he says through a full mouth.

My eyes narrow. "You got it on purpose, didn't you?"

His face lights up, and he nods enthusiastically.

"You don't even *like* sandwiches, do you?" I say.

Marty swallows. "I think they're efficient."

I roll my eyes. "Martin, dear, *please*. Someone who's worried about efficiency wouldn't be reading *War and Peace*. Tolstoy should've edited that monster down into a short story."

Marty pales visibly. "I'm going to pretend you didn't say that," he whispers.

"I tried to read it once myself. I got seven pages in before deciding war and peace were both interminably boring."

He swallows. "It really picks up after the first four hundred pages."

"I'm sure."

"Well," he starts, hesitates, before blurting: "I think Shakespeare is overrated." He waits for my reaction.

I shake my head sadly, because there is no accounting for poor taste. "Martin, dear Martin. 'We are such stuff as dreams are made on, and our little life is rounded with a sleep.'"

The words sound all wrong as they leave my lips, much sadder, more serious than I meant them to be. We're silent for a time. He adjusts his glasses, which are thicker now than they were before, despite the drugs the doctors inject into his eyes every month. He shoots me a look of feigned reproach. He reads, "'One step beyond that boundary line which resembles the line dividing the living from the dead lies uncertainty, suffering, and death. And what is there? Who is there?—there beyond that field, that tree, that roof lit up by the sun? No one knows, but one wants to know.'" He pauses, licks his lips. "'You fear and yet long to cross that line, and know that sooner or later it must be crossed and you will have to find out what is there, just as you will inevitably have to learn what lies on the other side of death. But you are strong, healthy, cheerful, and excited, and are surrounded by other such excitedly animated and healthy men.'"

He is expectant. I meet his gaze, and in his gaze I see the walls of Westing, equipped with state-of-the-art motion sensors, patrolled by guards. I see the fields and trees and roofs lit beyond the walls, the parents beyond them, parents whose letters Marty, unlike me, answers.

THE END TIME IS YOUR TIME

MAKE IT COUNT

Start BELIEVING today.
Wake up to a new TOMORROW.

This Message Brought to You by the
WESTING BELIEVERS

Meetings Every Thursday: Bullsworth Auditorium

Join us online at AwayWeGo.com/groups/believe

WHO WE TALK ABOUT
WHEN WE TALK ABOUT LOVE

After breakfast, I drop Marty off at the Westing Library, which looks like something out of Tolkien's Middle Earth, all towers and parapets. Inside, urinals and books are strictly segregated.

"I'll be in here for a while," Marty says.

"More of the Russians?"

He gives me a sheepish shrug. "You can never have enough dead Russians in your life."

"Got to go to work now," I say. "Might drop in to annoy you later, Martin dear."

I go to work in the sense that I show up three times a week for two hours a pop to get trained for a job I've yet to undertake. The money I make from that plus my requisite student stipend— provided by my parents—goes into an account. I can then buy foreign-made shirts and mugs with the Westing logo stamped onto their fronts—a gold *W* over an impressionistic rendition of Galloway Hall. Oh, yes, and alcohol, too. Alcohol most definitely. I don't know how it gets smuggled in, but I'm sure glad someone figured it out.

It was Alice's idea to become orientation leaders for the newsies, the incoming students that will be arriving in the fall. The only thing we're leaders of at the moment, however, is "community building" and listening studiously as administrative authorities lecture us on the dangers of drinking, drugs, and unprotected sex, presumably so we can pass all this information onto the newsies. Nobody ever bothers to mention the little matter of showing up as a name under DEPARTEES.

Today Alice and I are assigned to community-build the garbage out of the academic quad. We take it room by room, bin by bin.

"You wouldn't know a girl named Addie, would you?" she asks me.

Cold wells up inside me. "Umm, yeah. Why?"

"Addie and I have the same advisor, so we see each other sometimes, during his office hours. . . . She told me you're friends with her boyfriend. Zach, I think his name was. You do polo together. I didn't know we had polo."

The cold circulates through my body.

"Noah?"

"We watch vids of old polo games. From the library. Sometimes we climb onto each other's backs and pretend to be riding horses. Mostly guys, so it's pretty homoerotic, riding each other around. Zach's my favorite polo steed."

"I can never get a straight answer from you," she says, pretending to be cross.

Ha. A *straight* answer.

"I'm a complicated person," I explain.

She rolls her eyes. "But—so you know him?"

"Yes—umm, yeah. We're—friendly, yeah. We lived in Clover together. We had a race."

"A race? I thought you *hated* races."

"'Hate' is a strong word."

"When I mentioned you going out for track you gave me that thirty-minute lecture about how beating other people is a—"

"Contrived attempt at finding meaning in a nihilistic void

of nothing!" I finish, with enough glee that Alice shoots me a worried look.

"Yes, *that*," she says, and I can tell she's making a concerted effort at not rolling her eyes again.

"This race was different," I say, glancing out a window onto the academic quad. She looks at me strangely, like she's trying to read my expression. In the quad, a pair of students sit on a bench, smoking, a guy and a girl. I watch their lips move, invent their words: *I love you so much, Jenny. Oh, I love you so much, too, Michael. Look how happy we are. Let's make everyone who's not in love feel shitty about themselves. Give me a smooch. Smoochysmoochysmoochysmooch.*

"What about him?" I ask, finally. "Zach?"

"He's sick, Noah," she says, quiet. "I mean, *really* sick. Addie said she didn't know how much longer—she thought your favorite polo steed, he might be happy to see you."

"He asked for me?" My voice sounds too pained, too desperate. I don't know why, suddenly, I'm panicking. I've only *just* seen Zach. He told me about baby heirloom tomatoes. The key he gave me is heavy in my pocket.

"You should visit him, Noah. He's your *friend*. He deserves that."

I try not to look at Alice. "I've been meaning to," I say, which is not exactly a lie, but not exactly a truth either.

"If you want I could come with you. I don't know him, but—"

"No," I say, too quickly. I can tell she's hurt. "It's something I need to do alone. Anyway, it's not like we don't see each other. Polo Club's just on hiatus." Another half-truth. I don't tell her our hiatus has been going on for, like, eight months. I don't tell her we're waiting for Zach to fall sick, sick enough to be taken away. Then we'll find out. We'll find out where all the sick kids go.

"I know you don't want to hear this, but it could help to see someone," she says.

Aha. Of course. Enlisting me in Westing's counseling services is her latest Noah Salvation Initiative. Before this, she'd tried dragging me to chapel, then to Bible study, where I posed queries like "If God is omnipotent, why did he need to rest on the seventh day? Imagine if he'd powered through. We might've had unicorns." I was encouraged to limit my participation in future meetings.

"It could help you work through your feelings," she continues.

"You're right," I say. "I don't want to hear it."

Guilt simmers inside me. She and I take out the trash in silence after that. Once we finish with Gates, we move on to Lombardy. Maybe I'm feeling guilty for being brusque with her. Maybe I'm lonely. Maybe it's the tertiary care informational flyer I find under a chair in a corner of the room. Or maybe it's as simple as I don't want to pick up garbage anymore.

Regardless, I kiss her. My hands are inside her shirt, her right nipple hard under my thumb.

"Not here," she whispers.

"'Here,' 'there,' it's all arbitrary anyway."

In a world without objective meaning, in a world of cosmic emptiness, a lab table is as good as a bed.

But Alice doesn't understand.

"Not here," she insists, and breaks away from me.

With a sigh, I return to picking up trash.

. . .

Understanding Tertiary Care

SERVICES

- Memory and Physical Frailty Aid -
- Bathing and Grooming Aid -
- Incontinence Support -
- Medication Administration -
- Recreational Hour -
- Emotional and Spiritual Counseling -
- 24/7 Nurse-on-call -

RESIDENCES

- Spacious rooms -
- Large, bright windows -

DINING

- Three Chef-prepared Meals Daily -
- Personal Meal Delivery -

Each lakeside apartment houses three to five students. Apartment 112 belongs to me, Marty, and Alice. I wanted Zach to be our fourth, to apply with us at the end of spring semester, when all the new students ditch their obligatory newsie-year doubles and triples for suites, singles, and Lakeside Apartments. But Zach already had a single and anyway, it's hard to arrange living with someone if you never bring it up to him.

The mere thought makes me panicky.

In Alice's room, I press my lip to hers. The lake outside glistens in the bright of the afternoon, and my head is full of Zach. Alice breathes into my shoulder, the smell of garbage hanging onto us, faint but discernible, and there before me is the blue of Zach's eyes, the warmth of his hand on my shoulder. Afterward, lying naked in bed together, I watch her doze. My pants are on the floor by the bed.

I reach into a pocket and draw out the key.

How many times did Zach hold it?

I lean back onto the bed.

A quick glance at Alice assures me she's asleep, so I bring the key to my lips, pop it into my mouth, and taste the metal, and after a moment, something more, the faint imprint of his touch.

She wakes with her head on my chest. When she speaks into me it tickles. After two hours of garbage duty, I have to admit, that's nice. Nicer than sex, maybe. But I can't understand a word she says. I turn briefly away, pretend to rub at my mouth so I can spit the key into my palm.

"What?" I say.

"I said you seemed a little distracted. You get this faraway look in your eye."

"Is this a gentle way of critiquing my performance?"

"No," she says, too quickly. "You're not mad, are you?"

"For you not letting us do it on a lab table with a board full of chemistry equations as our background? Why would I be mad?"

"We have to keep it together, Noah," she says, tracing the outline of my ribs with her index finger. "Once you stop caring about where you have, well, you know, soon enough you stop caring who you have it with. Stop caring about anything at all. . ."

"But the nihilistic void of nothing—" I start to protest.

"—is not something I want to bring into bed with us," she says, elbowing me playfully.

I laugh. "Abuse!"

"You know," she says, after a time. "You know, I was thinking maybe we could have a picnic sometime soon. Next week, maybe. Get some sandwiches together and take them over to the lake. I know you love any excuse to eat sandwiches. We could ask Martin to come. What do you think?"

"Okay," I say.

I wrap my arms around her in a tight hug, and the metal of the key digs into my palm. But all I can think is that she is not Zach. She is not Zach she is not Zach she is not Zach, and I would rather be held than hold. It makes you feel like you add up to more than the nothingness inside you.

It makes you feel like you'll never go anywhere, and that is the only therapy I need.

I close my eyes with the hope that I'll dream of him.

DREAMS OF THE END

Noah knows the comet will hit.

In his final moments, he sits down to write a story.

But the blank sheets of paper taunt him.

To put words on paper is not a problem.

But the *right* words?

It used to be said that the Bible was the greatest book ever written. A myopically western-centric view, but, arrogance aside, the boldness of the claim, that is what appeals to Noah.

The libraries of the world are full of ancient books, populated by Gods and Heroes.

Are all these books holy, or are none of them?

Noah suspects the latter.

The blank pages on his desk leer at him.

His problem, he realizes, is that he wants to write a holy book, yet does not believe in the possibility of holiness. And if there is no possibility of holiness, why bother writing at all?

The answer to his question strikes him as suddenly as an accident.

He must write to save himself.

A YEAR BEFORE THE CATACLYSMIC, FIERY, KIND OF CLICHÉD END OF ALL THINGS (OR NOT)

THE END TIME IS YOUR TIME

Alice has always been trying to save me.

The bus to Westing was full of newsies from recovery centers all across Virginia.

I had a window seat, and Alice had the aisle seat right beside me. I was pretending to be asleep so I wouldn't have to exchange pleasantries, be pleasant.

The ride was long and bumpy, the outside world a thin windowpane away, which I would occasionally peek at, but there were soldiers on our bus, soldiers with guns. One of the soldiers sat across the aisle from Alice and me. He was in his early twenties, with faint blond wisps for a mustache and a rifle in his hands.

Alice reached out a hand. "Hi," she said, with a wide smile. "I'm Alice Witaker. I'm very pleased to meet you. What's your name?"

He stared at her like she had three heads.

"Not supposed to speak to you," he said finally. "You're cute and all, but I got my orders, and it's nothing personal or anything."

"Oh," Alice said, her hand wavering in the air. "Oh, okay. I understand. I wouldn't want you to get in trouble."

"It's nothing personal or anything," the soldier said, and turned away.

Alice looked crestfallen, so I pretended to wake up from my pretend sleep. I offered her my hand.

"Lucky for you I have no such orders," I said. "I'm Noah Falls."

Alice took my hand. "How was your nap, Noah Falls?" she asked, the hint of a reproach in her voice.

"It involved lots of sheep, Alice Witaker," I said.

"Are your dreams often farm-themed, Noah Falls?"

"Aren't yours?"

She cracked a smile.

"I'll take that as a yes," she said.

It was thanks to Alice that, soon after I arrived at Westing, I learned the world was going to end in a year's time. She dragged me to Bullsworth 112, where I sat in a circle of desks and listened to Morgan, president of the Believers, tell us about the comet Apep, her eyes wide and distant.

"—a mile wide," she was saying, "traveling thirty thousand miles per hour. It'll release as much energy as a one-million-megaton bomb."

She didn't mention the AwayWeKnow science articles in which NASA scientists put the odds of impact at one in ten thousand.

She said instead, that we shouldn't trust what we read on AwayWeKnow. After all, if kids knew the truth, they'd panic. Only two things can stand in the way of panic—belief, or ignorance.

"These are our last days. So what do we do? We live our lives as if the world depends on our actions. We be better people. We manifest a better reality. This is our test, our trial."

I could've filled in the rest for her. These last days are our tribulation, our means of lending our passing some semblance of meaning, our moment of self-definition in the light of the fires of Armageddon or whatever.

The fact that there was a chance the whole world,

everything anyone ever did, might end so *stupidly*—not a good chance, but still a chance—was all the proof I needed that there were no better realities to manifest, no great trials and tribulations. You just waited and waited to run into some shitty accident of nature. A rock, a germ, a falling tree. An apocalyptic asteroid that would destroy all life as you know it. A banana peel.

I tugged at the sleeve of Alice's dress.

She ignored me.

I continued tugging.

Finally, she sighed to let me know that I had prevailed, as I had known I would.

"Do you think," I whispered, "that our esteemed president has considered that the odds of The Great Cliché hitting the earth are about the same as winning big in Vegas and blowing it on—ha— blow, hookers, and penile enhancement? I believe in believing in nothing, but if you must believe in something, why not Vegas?"

"'The Great Cliché'," she echoed. "Oh my God, you can't even take the end of the world seriously."

"I am very serious about not taking anything seriously," I confirmed.

She studied me for a moment, with a doctor's unnerving intensity, before settling on a diagnosis: "You," she said, "are a *troll*."

I could hardly believe my ears. Girl picked up some Internet lingo, courtesy of AwayWeGo, and now insisted on transposing it to real-life situations, mainly those involving me.

"You're a *sheep*," I whispered, and instantly felt bad, wanted to take it back.

She rolled her eyes. "You and your sheep, Noah Falls."

"I have a dream, that one day, we will be judged, not on the basis of which farm animals we have in our dreams, but on how we choose to spend perfectly decent Friday nights."

"Troll," she reiterated, in case I hadn't gotten it the first time.

Just then the door to the room swung open, revealing a group of boys.

"Welcome, welcome!" Morgan said with grating enthusiasm as they picked their noisy way to the outskirts of our circle. We made room for them, and Morgan resumed her spiel, but after a few minutes, one of the newcomers proceeded to raise his hand. His hair was long, tied back into a ponytail. He wore an A-shirt that revealed painfully skinny arms. His three friends snickered to themselves as Ponytail fidgeted in his seat, waving his hand this way and that.

"I have a question. Miss! Miss President. Madame President!"

Morgan looked startled. "Yes?" she said, in a surprisingly meek voice.

"Madame President," he said. "You've been talking about belief and making things manifest, right? Well, see, what I was wondering, me and my friends—can we believe ourselves into bed with a girl? Believe and make it manifest? Is that how this thing works?"

"Because," another of the boys piped in, "and I intend no disrespect to this noble organization or its professed goals, but, personally, I would much rather expend my energies toward that eventuality, especially in light of the apparent imminence of the world's end."

"He's a virgin," Ponytail said of his friend. "You can tell by the way he talks."

The Believers put their warm, fuzzy feelings about manifesting better realities in honor of killer comets to the side for the moment to tell the four intruders that "We're trying to do something useful with our lives, so if you don't like it, go die in a ditch."

"No, you know what? These guys have converted me," Ponytail said. "We manifest our realities, so I guess my sister died 'cause she's a little bitch. Only a bitch dies from organ failure when she's thirteen, right?"

The meeting was beginning to look more and more like a future crime scene. I grabbed Alice's hand and dragged her toward the door. Morgan, practically in tears, barred our path, hastily offering us a small bucket full of pins that read "BELIEVERS: The End Time Is Your Time."

As I took a pin I noticed a red mark on the side of Morgan's neck. Who'd put it there? Had she lectured him on the power of "Positive Actualization" in the face of the apocalypse? Why wasn't he here, manifesting a reality that involved standing up for her?

"Thank you for the pin," I said.

Any desire to challenge Morgan was gone.

She just wanted to *believe* she added up to something so she could sleep easier, because going away was a lonely business, and yes, it made you feel better to think the world was going away with you. Who could blame Morgan, really, for wanting to sleep easier?

That was why you had to choose the right bedtime stories. The director with her grand convocation day speeches about Westing's singular purpose. The students working in the library, doing research for teachers, volunteering, going to clubs, whispering theories about where the sick kids go, whispering that tertiary care clinics involving bathing and grooming support were just a cover-up for secret government labs where mad scientists cut Bobby Fisher from econ into pieces in order to cure PPV and save the rest of us, like in this AwayWeWatch flick called *The Treatment Program*. They pretended that the outside world wasn't actively trying to forget us, hadn't boxed us in, limited our Internet access to a grand total of one site, limited our cell phone communication to calling kids who lived down the hall from us, even as our parents sent us letters and micro-transactions through AwayWeGame in the form of Pirate World booty or Age of Rome florins. Most of all, kids pretended all of this *stuff*, these *activities* they did, the grades they got, actually mattered.

Bullsworth Hall, Room 112
Thursday, September 15th, 8 PM

The Westing Believers Club is for students who are interested in ~~making~~ *wholesome sex* ~~the most of their time at Westing.~~ We will discuss the power of positive thinking and engage in motivational excercises, all while getting to know each other ~~in a warm and friendly environment!~~ *intimately*

Newsie are especially encouraged to attend!

Upcoming activies will include student speakers, a book club, Fun Friday Game Nights, and ~~more!~~ WITH AFOREMENTIONED STUDENT SPEAKERS   WHAT'S UR # ?

I feel left out :(←

Sex
on my face pls & thnx   *mine too!!*

Please Come ∧   **All are Welcome**

Contact Club President, Morgan Cartwright, for more information at:

mcartwright@awaywemail.com

SILVERWARE IN THE SKY

An hour or two after the Believer meeting, Alice and I had one of those which-way-should-the-toilet-paper-go arguments where the toilet paper is a metaphor for. Pretty. Much. *Everything*. We were in the gardens behind Galloway, bickering like a married couple even though we'd only known each other for a week.

It began with the stars.

Her: You've *never* seen the Big Dipper?

Me: I don't really get the name.

Her: The name?

Me: What the hell. Is a *dipper*. Do you mean spoon? The big spoon in the sky?

Her: Why are you so mad?

Me: Because—waste of a night, Alice. And now you want to talk about imaginary silverware in the sky.

Her: You need people, Noah. You need hope and friends and something to do other than drink and whatever else I saw you doing the other night, and I'm sorry if spending an evening with a friend and a bunch of people who want to make the most of the time that they have was so *dreadful*—

Me: You don't actually *believe* that shit? (I couldn't resist.)

Her: And what if I did believe that, as you say, *shit*? Would it be so terribly bad, Noah? To have some hope? And some friends? And something to do other than drink? It's like Director Bajwa said on convocation day—you wouldn't know, seeing as you weren't there—

Me: Ha. Ouch.

Her: —we have a purpose, here.

Me: I get it, you want me to seize the day, grab life by the horns. But the Big Dipper is just a bunch of burning gas and you know what, Alice? Grabbing the bull by the horns is actually a really bad idea, unless you're a professional bull wrangler. And even then, given the mortality rate of professional bull wrangling, I would suggest looking into other career options. I hear floristry is booming.

Her: You're being impossible.

Her: Who knows how many more months we have, Noah? How many more months *I* have? So if we care about someone, or think we could learn to care—

Me: We've known each other for, like, a week, Alice.

Her: I know. I'm—I'm sorry. I'm just scared. I didn't mean to—I don't want to pressure you. It's just that we don't have, who knows how much time we have. . . .

I should've told her that time wasn't the issue. Our week might as well have been a year. But I'd lost my parents, I'd lost Alex, and I needed an anchor. I needed someone to need me, to lend me weight, I needed a reason not to simply disappear, Great Cliché or no.

Me: I'm going for a run.

The faster I ran, the more I ached, the easier it was to pretend that I was a physical thing, that I had weight and solidity, *a body*, and that this body had somewhere to run away to, that it was worth running at all.

Westing News

Transcript of Director Bajwa's Convocation Address at Westing Academy

(cont. from page 1)

Every day, we face renewed criticism of our cause. We here at Westing try to shield our students from these realities because we want to give you a semblance of normalcy. But these well-meaning intentions should not contribute to a warped understanding of the world in which you reside. To paraphrase Representative Gilbert from California, quoted this morning in the *New York Times*: Why waste millions upon millions of taxpayer dollars educating a handful of kids who'll never work and never pay taxes?

We are here because we believe the value of an education is not based on utility to society. Westing is an experiment founded on the notion that the value of an education is in its ability to elevate and liberate the soul. We seek to transform the recovery process, fostering partnerships with AwayWeGo to facilitate connections and interpersonal learning while at Westing, and a local, stringently vetted tertiary clinic to ensure the best possible hospice experience post-Westing.

There are many who want to bury this, bury *all of you* as quickly and efficiently as possible. Many who would send you to glorified internment camps, prisons, because there are too many of you, because it is too expensive to provide for you, or so they say. We are the voice that says no, for there are Michelangelos here. There are Sapphos here. But we need your cooperation. You must work. You must produce. And you must stay within these walls. You must contribute to the success of the Westing experiment, so that someday, all youths in recovery will have the quality of life you now enjoy. ■

HOW TO IDENTIFY A
HIGH-CALIBER HUMAN BEING

I spent the rest of September alternating between raging drunkenness and hangovers so severe the mere thought of movement prompted waves of nausea. To be sober was to miss Alex, to *act* was to miss Alex. It was so easy to lose people. We were all so weightless and insubstantial. To keep myself rooted to the ground, I kept the shots coming, night after night, made intimate friends with toilet seats, rising past noon to wash away the stench of vodka as hot water pooled in the drain at my feet, until one day, I realized halfway into my shower that I'd forgotten my room key. All newsies got stuck in doubles or triples for their first year at Westing, but my roommate Marty had already left for class.

"Locked out this early in the semester?" a voice said, just as I'd been contemplating whether or not to try to bust my door open.

I turned, and felt like the disparate pieces of me had suddenly congealed into a person again, a person whose stomach promptly lurched into his throat. The voice belonged to a boy of sixteen or so, lean and tan and strangely happy. The words escaped my mouth before I had a chance to think twice about them: "No," I said. "I just like standing outside my door for hours on end. It's a pastime."

He laughed. "You *do* have that practiced aura about you," he said with a nod. His eyes were blue, like he had a splash of water in them. "An aura of togetherness."

My turn to laugh. Aside from my current key-less predicament, my only form of attire at the moment was a blue-and-yellow polka dot towel, my eyes were so bloodshot it looked like I'd smoked three pounds of weed in the shower, and to top it all off, I wasn't exactly sure what day it was.

The very picture of togetherness.

"Today is a Tuesday, right?" I asked.

He tried not to grin and failed. He extended a hand. "I'm Zach, by the way. Zachary, if you like. I'm the student council vice president and self-appointed-newsie-helper-person-dude, God help you all. I like your towel."

"Is it Wednesday?" I tried, and felt guilty for flirting. I'd been away from Richmond, from Alex, for three weeks. . . . Was that all it took? Three weeks? And then there was Alice. I'd been avoiding her, but couldn't she see that we'd never make each other happy?

"Better I don't answer that," he said with a wink. "You'll need to find security. They can bust down your door for you! I can show you where they are."

"It's okay," I said, because I wanted to leave Zach, to prove to Alex I remembered him.

He placed a hand on my bare shoulder and said, "Nonsense, kid. It is my solemn duty to help you. You are, after all, my constituent, and besides, I'll need your vote in the next election."

So we rode the elevator down to Clover's ground floor, together in that cramped space. I couldn't help fantasizing about the elevator getting stuck, the lights going dark.

No such luck.

We arrived on the ground floor without incident, at which point he led me outside, all the way to the campus security office in Galloway.

"You'll do well here; I can tell by your towel," he said by way of parting, and pressed a hand to my bare shoulder again.

"You can tell a lot about a person from his towel," I managed.

"*Exactly,*" he said, and beamed at me. "You are a human of high caliber, kid." He tapped a finger to his temple to indicate his knowledge of such things. The temple-tap turned into a good-bye wave.

Before I could figure out how to make him stay, he was gone, and I felt light and airy again, like I was a boy made up of strands of wind.

THE SKY IS FALLING AND I LIKE IT

I was trying to reform.

After spending my first solid month at Westing married to alcohol, I'd set myself to reading numbers 10 and 51 of the Federalist Papers in Galloway's Victorian-style lavender parlor as rain drummed against the roof, like a good, model newsie. I could make out the Galloway lawn and the empty parking lot from where I sat. The sky had darkened and the last of the teachers' cars had rolled through security at the main gate, a funny name seeing as it was the *only* gate.

I glanced at my assignment, due tomorrow.

Please devote 3-5 pages to discussing how democratic the framers intended our original constitution to be.

What I had so far: "Contrary to popular belief, not very."

It was difficult to write, when it seemed like my thoughts wouldn't matter much to anyone, when they didn't even matter much to me.

A tap on the shoulder made me jump. Numbers 10 and 51 spilled out of my lap onto the polished hardwood. My laptop almost went down, too; I barely caught it in time.

"Bit jumpy there, eh, kid?" Zach asked as he bent over and began to scoop my papers up. I started to help him, but he said, "I got this, no worries."

He handed me the stack with dripping hands. He was soaked, dark hair plastered to his head, had on a T-shirt that read: *I react to chemistry.*

"Now, Noah, I haven't seen you in all of forever," he said as he plopped down next to me, put a wet arm around my shoulder. I didn't know whether to lean into it or to pull away, so I stayed limp and unmoving. "What I want to know is," he went on, "well—how are you? Any complaints? Grievances? Issues you're too shy to take up with the administration?"

"Now that you mention it, there's no toilet paper in the bathroom—"

"Because," he interrupted, "that's what the secretary is for. Or the treasurer. Or the president. Noah, do not hesitate to bother them. Consider this permission granted. That's what they're for, and *God*, I don't particularly like them, so I won't pretend I won't get a certain satisfaction out of it—Noah, I know I'm pretty but please, we need to concentrate. There are times for drifting off into my eyes and there are times for serious business." He gave me a stern look. "This is a time for serious business."

"You're completely wet."

"Oh, that," he said, as if he hadn't noticed it, but he withdrew his arm. "I took a jog in the rain. Was hoping I'd catch pneumonia. So far no luck. I think I'm going back out there to try again. Care to join me?"

"Pneumonia together?" I said. All thoughts of reforming myself into a better student vanished.

He nodded. "What better way for an elected officer to bond with his constituency?"

"By advocating for their best interests, à la toilet paper in the bathroom on the—"

He scoffed. "We're not running a socialist utopia here, Noah. There will be no redistribution of toilet paper. We must trust in the market." Then, "Are you coming, or am I going to have to go right on out there and get pneumonia all on my lonesome?"

I nodded to my computer, my papers. "Give me a minute?"

I met him outside Galloway's main entrance, under the canopy, my heart hammering as if I'd already run three marathons, and as soon as he saw me push through the door, he took off into the rain, yelling over his shoulder, "WE'RE RACING!"

I chased after him, splashing through the wet, down paved paths, and then the dirt trails. Past the Wellness Center and the residential quad. Then up a trail that led us by the Lakeside Apartments on our left, the wall on our right, the lamps along the wall lit in the rainy dusk.

He was fast, faster than me.

The rain fell hard against my skin, the dark in the horizon punctuated here and there by rumbling undercurrents of light. I heaved breaths in the lulls between distant peals of thunder, and as I drew up beside him he winked at me, sped up, pushed himself harder. There was a massive puddle up ahead; my sneakers squelched with every step through it and the mud left splotches against my legs. I knew if I looked behind, I'd see a trail of footprints, mine and his, side by side; I knew if I looked back I'd see the rain falling into the lake water in a thousand thousand places, the lake connected to the sky by strips of water, everything was water, and it seemed ridiculous now, the idea of my life not mattering, the idea that I was nothing.

I was the rain.

I was the lake.

I was the ground beneath my own feet.

I was full of everything.

I came back to my senses when I saw Zach breaking away. We'd passed the lake and were on the slick cobblestones of the forest path that ran behind Galloway, in the shadow of the evergreens, and I pushed harder. We were running like there was a ribbon waiting for us somewhere, anywhere, until finally, the cafeteria peeked into view, and I knew we were headed for the steps, but I couldn't beat him, and that's when he slowed.

Almost imperceptibly, but enough for me to catch up, enough for us to reach the steps together, and when we did he threw his arms up exultantly. Somehow we were hugging each other.

"God," he said, breaking away to stare off somewhere, then at me. "This calls for some hot chocolate."

Of course, the cafeteria was closed by this time, so we had to make our way back to the Academy Café in the rear of Galloway. We waited in line at the cashier with our cups, trailing water from our clothes, our hair. The cashier raised his eyebrows at us.

"I don't have any clean clothes," I realized aloud. I'd been meaning to do the laundry today.

Zach hesitated, his gaze flicked down and away. Then his eyes met mine: splashes of water, clouds, racing in the wet.

"I can spare you some," he said.

I was not going to write that paper. I was not going to write that paper. My delinquency had never made me happier.

I trudged beside him through the rain in the direction of the residential quad, holding my hot cup. In his room, I suddenly realized how wet and dirty I was. "Radiator's warm," he suggested, and coughed. "We're actually going to get pneumonia, though," he said with a slight frown.

"Here." He set his shoes and socks by the radiator, offered me a nightshirt and a pair of sweatpants to change into. He stripped out of his own shirt and jeans without a glance at me, revealing bronze skin, threw them on top of the radiator.

It made me stupidly happy, how well I fit into his clothes. I toweled my face off, any lingering wet on my body, and then we sat cross-legged next to the radiator, beside our sodden shoes and dripping clothes. I sipped my hot chocolate. The silence deepened, but we were close, our legs almost touching, until I pushed mine against his, gently. He set his empty cup down and I stretched out on the floor beside him. My hand found his; he let me hold it.

His leg brushed against my head and I pressed my cheek to his thigh, stared up at him.

Alex had pushed me away. Had he found someone to replace me?

But I couldn't think about Alex now.

I pushed myself up, and into Zach. He closed his eyes and I kissed him. We tried to fit our arms around each other, our bodies into each other.

"You taste like chocolate," he said pensively.

He brushed a leg against mine. We stayed like that for a minute or an hour, and it was uncomfortable, but also the best. Alice seemed strangely distant, not even real. We weren't together; I'd barely seen her since our first week at Westing, but she'd be hurt. Was it my fault she'd be hurt? A voice in my head insisted: *yes*.

"As much as I don't want to move—" I started.

"Because you're drifting into my eyes—"

"Yes, that. As much as I don't want to, my whole body is numb. If only there were a more comfortable place for two boys to lie."

He tousled my hair, which nearly killed me.

"Very sly," he said. "If only all my constituents were so subtle."

"Mention your constituents. One. More. Time. Zach."

I pulled both of us up, then pushed him gently onto his bed with a sheepish grin. I turned the lights off and jumped onto the bed after him, hit my head on the wall, and laughed.

"I'm so awkward," I said as I slid under the covers and lay facing him.

The brush of his hair against my forehead made me feel real.

I wanted to tell him I liked that he said *God* all the time, and that he had led me on a race through the rain, that he would've won, that he'd let it be a tie, that his boxers were blue, that he smelled like clean clothes and rain, that he had a radiator, that he was sick, that he existed at all, that there was a world with Zach in it, that I could reach out and touch him, feel that he, too, was real.

I wanted to do more than just lie there, but I couldn't.

He might say no.

He might push me away.

Before he fell asleep, he whispered into my ear, "By the way."

"Uh-huh."

"I'm starting a club."

"Of course you are."

"I want you to be in it." He paused. "It's Polo."

"Uh," I said. "Like, with horses?"

"Don't worry about trivialities, Noah."

And then he was snoring into my ear.

POLO

I dragged my roommate Marty along to Polo Club's first meeting, without telling him what I was dragging him to.

"It's a surprise," I explained.

"*Noah.*"

"Oh, come on. Hurry up," I said, cutting across the Galloway lawn in the direction of the academic quad.

He sighed theatrically, lagging behind. "All right."

"You won't regret it. I swear."

When we got to Lombardy 207, we saw written across the board in neat, bold letters:

POLO CLUB

Marty turned to me, eyes wide behind his glasses. "*Polo?*" he spluttered.

"That was my reaction, too."

"The sort with—*horses?*"

"That was *my* reaction, too!"

Before Marty could adequately translate the exasperation on his face into words, Zach grabbed a piece of crumbling chalk and wrote a question that knocked everyone's breath away.

What is 'going away'?

And a second.

Where do we 'go' when we 'go away'?

"We suspect, we speculate, we hear rumors," Zach said, gesticulating at the front of the room, the same Zach whose hair had brushed against my forehead. He wore a shirt that read: *Earth Science Rocks*, which nearly killed me. "But we don't *know* for sure. Polo Club is about knowledge. We're not going to be like F.L.Y. We're not going to demonstrate, or write editorial letters. We're not going to go on hunger strikes in Galloway. We're not even going to be an official organization. Our first rule is discretion. And the first thing we need is a plan of escape, a fail-safe—"

"You can't be serious," a blond boy near the front said. "What are we even talking about? Even if we could get out—I mean— we're quarantined for a reason. You want to get more kids sick?"

"Houston all over again," someone else muttered, and there were murmurs of assent.

"We're out in the middle of nowheresville, Vermont," Zach said, his splash-blue eyes searching for a friendly face, resting briefly on mine. I winked, and he blushed slightly. "As long as we don't go near other people we'll be fine," he continued. "Look, what I'm saying is—there are fourteen of us here. The woods are nearby. We could survive with fourteen people. Organize ourselves. Make shelters. Gather fruit. Hunt. Fish. God knows what else."

"I heard the guards at the main gate have guns," Marty said into my ear.

If I made it through the guards at the main gate, stowed away in the trunk of a car, the way Jane did to bypass a Vanguard checkpoint in *Firewalkers*—which I'd read in lieu of Faulkner the other day—then hiked through the woods, down the highways, across state lines, back to my home in Richmond, Virginia, would I knock on a worn door with flaking red paint, listen to the steps echo from inside as the wood of the porch creaked beneath me only to have a strange woman open the door, holding a child in her arms? I tried to picture her face and drew a blank. But I could hear the gentle currents of her voice, the swell of her laughter. I had no idea what she was saying, but sometimes, when it got quiet, and I was alone, going for a run, I could hear her, *Mom*, though I could never make out her words. I knew nostalgia wasn't good, wasn't healthy. Digging up the past was like digging up the dead, and my NAAP score had singled me out as a kid who left what's buried in the ground where it belonged, high-performing and well-adjusted, like everyone else here, and so I was rewarded with a campus full of castles and stained-glass windows while kids who got diagnosed in their later years, kids who were "troubled," kids who remembered their parents, rumor had it, were packed into improvised mass recovery clinics in Wyoming where they entered tertiary stage within a few scant years of diagnosis.

I had long given up on the possibility of hearing—*actually hearing*—Mom again.

"How many of us know how to do any of that at all?" said Grace, meaning hunting, fishing, evading bears. "I mean, gosh, I've always loved nature, I've always had what you call a green thumb and everything, flowers budding, plants sprouting, but what about everyone else?" Grace was completely sincere. We had twentieth-century American lit together, where the fact that she hadn't done any of the readings did not dissuade her from volunteering her opinion on issues ranging from Atticus's parenting philosophy to Carver's use of color in passages of great and terrible middle-American sadness (i.e., his whole canon). She was also the captain of the girl's rugby team and had more muscle mass in her left arm than I had in my whole body.

"But that's exactly the point." Zach bit his lip. A note of desperation had entered his voice. "It's a fail-safe. There are books on this sort of thing. We have the whole library. Look—

if we work together, divide the labor, we can figure out how to live out there. But the point of Polo isn't escape. Escape is a last resort. The point of Polo is to figure out what happens. Westing's not perfect, but we're happier here than we would be out there—"

"Without meds we wouldn't last long," Marty said, quietly.

"The escape plan is about giving us a choice," Zach said, his shoulders, his whole body tense. He massaged his temples with one hand, as if the novelty of this business had worn off and it was now all giving him a headache. "For our entire lives we've never been given a choice. I'm not talking about living in some city, exposing other people. What I'm saying is—we can't talk or visit friends at other recovery centers. Our news is filtered through AwayWeGo, even our news about why we only get news from AwayWeGo *is filtered through AwayWeGo*. And nobody tells us exactly *what happens* when they take us away, just stuff about tertiary clinics, those terrible flyers, spacious rooms and bright windows—you guys don't actually *believe* the flyers? You guys don't actually believe, palliative support and grooming and bathroom aid and then that's *it*?"

The kids in the room looked unconvinced, so I spoke up. "We've all heard things. We never hear from anyone who's taken away. Why? Haven't you guys wondered?"

Zach's features softened. He shot me a look of thanks.

"Yo, what I heard?" an extra-large-sized boy in a polo shirt piped up, between sips of orange soda. I was pretty sure his name was Nigel. He was so white he glowed in the dark and had an IQ of 157, or so he claimed. In our first week at Westing he drank half a liter of vodka, then got into a naked brawl with a door, which, incidentally, the door won. "I heard they get meds tested on them at those tertiary places. Experimentals. Probably half the time the cure's what croaks you up."

"Apes will only get you so far," Melanie, an Asian girl who dressed all in black and bit the last guy who tried to kiss her, said. "Their immune systems are much stronger than ours. If you're going to find a cure, human trials are a necessity." I was pretty sure she'd described the general plot of *The Cure*, an AwayWeWatch Top Ten Thrillers of the Year pick, but that didn't make me any less excited.

"Something's off," Zach said, summoning everyone's attention. "It's up to us to figure out what. And if we need to escape. . ."

Escape.

Zach and I could escape together.

We could go home.

I held on to the thought.

Katrina Mackey:
The Girl Whose Death Transformed Westing

Former lacrosse star Katrina Mackey was diagnosed with PPV at the age of fourteen, the summer before her sophomore year of high school at Elford High in Albany, New York. She was admitted to Westing but took her own life a mere month and a half after matriculation, following a campaign of cyber-bullying that continued post-mortem, with vicious comments from former classmates at Elford High accumulating on a tribute page set up by her friends at Westing. The comments referenced the events of the Houston quarantine, which had taken place several weeks prior.

"I'm sorry for what happened down in Houston, that I am, but it doesn't have a thing to do with our daughter, no, it doesn't," Mr. Mackey told *Good Morning America* shortly after his daughter's death.

The Mackeys have since divorced, but almost a decade later, they still do not know how anyone could have done such a thing.

"What kind of a person bullies a sick child? I don't care if they had family in Houston. They should know better," Mrs. Mackey said.

Katrina Mackey had been suffering from depression even before her PPV diagnosis, but her parents reported she'd made friends at Westing and was looking forward to trying out for the Westing lacrosse team in the spring. The Mackeys believe the taunts from former classmates pushed her over the edge.

In response to the events in Houston and the death of Katrina Mackey, Congress passed the Safe Recovery Act, which reformed contact between youths in recovery and the uninfected.

After Polo's first meeting, Zach demanded to know how he'd done. We sat together on a bench next to the library while students played Frisbee in the academic quad beneath a purple-orange sky. I tried to put into words how happy I was, that the boy whose bed I'd shared wanted to lead us all home, and also how wrong it felt, to be so happy while sitting on a memorial dedicated to a girl named Alexandra Cheung.

All the benches at Westing were dedicated to the memory of kids who'd gone away.

"Give me a rating," he said. "On a scale of one to ten."

I bumped my knee into his. "Terrible."

"I know. I know. I *know*." He brushed a hand through his hair. "God, they were looking at me like I was downright crazy."

"I helped," I said.

"You did."

"Because you were *bombing*. I mean, like, *nosediving*. I mean, like—"

"Dive-bombing!" he added excitedly. "Totally." He bumped me with his knee.

"Soooo," I said. "Wanna dive-bomb into your bed?"

"So sly," he said.

"Right?"

"So subtle."

"*Right?*"

He hesitated. "Not tonight, okay?" he asked softly.

I hid my hurt with an "Okay" and whipped out my phone. Alice had invited me to a movie night in Violet Hall. I'd been avoiding her, but now I messaged to ask if it was too late to take her up on her offer.

She texted back in record time:

come quiccckkk, it's only just starting. i saved u a seat :) :) :)

FRONT FOR THE LIBERATION OF YOUTHS IN RECOVERY

Think you're free?

Then WHY are your e-mails, texts, and phone conversations monitored?

WHY is your Internet access restricted?

WHY can't you call your family and friends outside?

WHY are you trapped behind motion-sensing walls?

Think you're free?
Think again.

"We declare our right on this earth . . . to be a human being, to be respected as a human being, to be given the rights of a human being in this society, on this earth, in this day, which we intend to bring into existence by any means necessary."

—Malcolm X (assassinated in 1965)

A FEATHER ON PLUTO

Zach and I both had towels distinguishing us as humans of high caliber wrapped around our waists. The bathroom mirror was flecked with toothpaste.

Zach brushed his teeth, spat his toothpaste out. "You leave your room open this time?"

"No idea," I said, trying not to stare. "I'm functioning at twenty-five percent capacity right now. I need at least three cups of coffee before short-term memory comes online."

"I prefer tea," he said. "Or hot chocolate," he added with a wink.

A week or so had passed since Polo Club's first meeting. I'd refrained from texting, or messaging him on AwayWeGo, at great expense to my sanity—if I ignored him, he would realize he needed me, and in a world so full of shadows that flickered and were gone, I needed to be needed, to believe I had more substance than that. While waiting for him to come around, I'd busied myself with busying myself. Marty had asked me to audition for a play he'd written, which the Westing Theater Troupe was putting on in April, and all my time whispering lines to myself at Richmond had paid off.

"So, I assume my speech at Polo Club—"

"Your *rousing* speech," I corrected.

He nodded with enthusiasm. "I assume my rousing speech— thank you again, by the way—"

"You're welcome."

"—has been the obvious highlight of your Westing experience so far?"

"Not really," I said, with as straight a face as I could manage. I took a shy step toward him.

"Wow." He laughed, set his toothbrush down. He crossed his hands over his chest. "Honesty isn't always the best policy, Noah." He averted his eyes as he said that last part.

"Polo's too bourgeois for me," I explained. "I prefer acting. How do you feel about Romeo and Juliet? Star-crossed lovers and all that."

"I think amorous relationships between the electors and the elected are complicated enough without involving astrophysics. The electors are all ra ra ra twinkle dinkle little star ra ra ra—"

"Sorry," I said, cupping a hand to my ear. "What was that?"

"Ra ra ra twinkle dinkle little star ra ra ra," he said to humor me, and chewed at the inside of his lip as I chanced yet another step. He was the only boy I'd ever met who wouldn't actually look at you while flirting.

"Did I tell you I'm going to be Peter Pan?" I asked him.

Zach raised his eyebrows, so I explained about how Marty had won the annual MacGregor Playwriting Contest for *Away We Go*, his modern take on *Peter Pan*, and had offered me the main part.

Zach squinted, tilted his head to the side, gave me a thumbs-up. "I've often thought about what Peter Pan would look like if he were a Polo-playing Westing student brushing his teeth in one of our bathrooms, and I have to say, you're *exactly* like I pictured him, right down to both your chest hairs. The vice president is invited to the grand premiere, right? 'Cause if said vice president hadn't saved you from being locked out, why, we would have proceeded down a completely different causal line. Butterfly effect, you know."

"I could've ended up as Wendy."

He tapped his temple a couple times, to indicate he'd thought of everything.

Just then the bathroom door swung open, and Nigel stepped through.

Nigel glanced from me to Zach to me.

I realized with horror that I had a raging erection poking at one of the yellow polka dots decorating my towel. My stomach compressed into a single dense point—a black hole, an infinitely dense polka dot of sexual frustration.

Nigel looked at my face, then at my towel.

I looked at his face, then at my towel.

"Yo brosefs, there's some fun been going on up in *here!*" he said, clapping us both on our shoulders. "*Somebody's* for real gonna need a new towel soon." He threw himself into a stall, and proceeded to narrate his history of irritable bowel syndrome, but we weren't listening.

"Come to dorm tea this Thursday?" Zach asked me, but didn't wait for my response.

He'd pushed through the exit, gone, and I was left thinking about Earl Grey versus English breakfast.

"Yo, brosef," Nigel said from his stall. "Hand me some toilet paper? I'm out over here, man, and these here are about to be some desperate times. I can feel it in my bowels."

My phone buzzed in my pocket.

It was Zach.

Get there early. Sofa spots limited. ;]

I spent the next day and a half thinking about that winky face.

I had never met someone who used a bracket in lieu of a parenthesis.

• • •

Who knew Thursday Tea nights in Clover were the place to be? Faces sipping from mugs crowded the multipurpose room. I'd arrived early enough to guarantee myself a coveted sofa spot, thanks to Zach.

"I would've defunded them, *too*," a wiry blond-haired guy named Matt said of F.L.Y.'s op-ed in the *Westinger*, in which F.L.Y. advocated students rushing the main gate. The editorial came out this Monday. By today, the student council had defunded F.L.Y. and threatened to do the same to the *Westinger* if the editorial board didn't resign.

"We didn't have a choice," Zach said, rubbing at his eye. "The administration would've replaced the whole student council if we hadn't yes-sirred along with it."

"That's some workers-of-the-world-unite shit they were on about," a guy in a beanie said, radiating the scent of weed. Zach smiled at him encouragingly, so he went on, "which is *fucked up*, right? But if we don't have free speech, then what's the admin hiding, know what I mean? When I called my parents on the home hotline"—this prompted groans from all around. Nobody wanted to admit they believed in secret hotlines that connected youths in recovery directly to their parents—"I *did*, okay?" the guy in the beanie insisted. "And they told me—"

"They loved you?" someone suggested.

"That the hope of hearing your voice again was their only reason for living?" another piped in.

"*Hey*. Fuck you guys. Matt's voice is my reason for living," said a third.

Laughter.

"Guys, don't be cruel," Zach said, leaning forward slightly, so his elbows rested on his knees. He averted his eyes. People shifted uncomfortably, tried to stifle their grins. "Matt's a nice kid, and has excellent taste in tea."

"All I'm saying," Matt said, gesticulating wildly, ignoring Zach's kindness, "is maybe I don't want to be a lab rat with my last memories downloaded on a chip that some fat-ass gets to pop in his fat head so he can whack off to my girlfriend while they dissect my body for the benefit of science so some rich dude's Pomeranian can have my spleen and live to a hundred seventy-three doggie years. I mean, Jesus holy-in-heaven Christ. Free speech, man. My parents are fucking *taxpayers*."

Everyone laughed, then promptly forgot Matt and his beanie had ever existed, except me, because Zach had called Matt a *kid*.

I was supposed to be Zach's kid.

"You should've resigned instead of going along with it," a girl with blue highlights said, her eyes boring into Zach.

"Instead of being the admin's *bitches*," Matt said, and I wanted to punch him.

Zach paled a bit, then smiled. I was about to come to his defense when he said, "As the vice president, I advised the president to do just that. I said it would make a strong statement. He accused me of ulterior motives. Clearly, someone's forgotten his obligation to the people."

Just like that, he had everyone laughing; everyone's faces, it seemed, were fixed in orbit around him, even the girl with blue highlights had softened, and I felt cold and distant and free-floating, like a feather on Pluto—why had he invited me here, only to ignore me?

I brought my mug to my lips and drank. I went from cold to hot, my forehead sweaty, my shirt sticking to my back. Why did Matt have to bring up that shit about becoming a lab experiment? I'd read on AwayWeKnow about scientists from places like Harvard and MIT trying to save kids by preserving their memories, their identities in code, ones and zeroes. There was an AwayWeRead book, *The Peter Pan Project*, about a scientist at UC Berkeley who uploads one infected child's memories into a robot which can then answer simple yes or no questions about the dead boy's childhood, his favorite candy (Twizzlers), his favorite sport (soccer).

On the AwayWeRead *Peter Pan Project* discussion forums, *anonymoose* had speculated about digitized memories being sold to the highest bidder, any adult on the outside who wanted to relive their adolescence, while *latexluvin* added that PPV was an Illuminati population-control plot. *Kyle2.0* asked if androids dream of electric sheep.

I thought of a robot Zach, answering my questions.

Did we meet at Westing? Yes.

Did we share the same bed? Yes.

Do you love me? ...

Are you still in there? ...

Zach? ...

I couldn't breathe. Every moment I spent with Zach I wanted to both be nowhere else and anywhere else. I wanted to feed him strawberries and jump out the nearest window. I was almost at the exit when he caught me by the arm. I wasn't expecting the touch and briefly experienced a mild form of cardiac arrest.

"Hey," he said, "didn't know there were going to be so many people tonight. Maybe because we have Earl Grey this time?"

I tried to play along. "That's why I came."

"To watch me drink Earl Grey?"

"Yes," I said. I didn't have the energy to lie.

He frowned in thought. "You've been quiet tonight."

It hadn't occurred to me till now. I thought to apologize for not coming to his defense.

"Groups," I started. "Groups aren't really my thing. I get lost in them."

A girl heading for the exit cleared her throat. Zach and I stepped out into the hall to let her pass.

"I don't know who to be in a group," I went on, staring after her. "I know who to be when it's one on one. Or when someone's written the lines. I just think we're the most ourselves when we're alone."

He bit his lip, glanced inside where people were still milling. Our spots on the sofa had been taken.

"How 'bout a game of pool?" he offered.

So we took the elevator down to the basement. In the game room's poor light, Zach assembled the balls into a neat triangle.

"None of that stripes and solids polarizing factionizing nonsense," he said. "Why divide the balls into opposing groups? God, why create false dichotomies? They're all balls. Let them be united in their common ball-dom. Let's just hit them in. But if you hit the eight ball in, we both lose, obviously."

"Obviously," I said, with zero idea of the actual rules.

So I aimed for the eight ball. After I'd hit it in three times, he asked me if I was okay.

I leaned against the table, regarding Zach's silhouette in the half-light. "I was thinking about what Matt said. And about Polo. Do you think something's going on at Westing?"

What I wanted to ask, but didn't: Why did you invite *me* to Polo, and not Matt?

For a time, Zach didn't speak. "There's got to be, Noah," he said, softly. "It's terrible, but I want there to be. Is that terrible?" He spoke more quickly, grew more excited. "I'd rather have my head sliced open and my memories extracted and sold on AwayWeSellTheDeepestMostIntimatePartsOfYourSoul than just, nothing. There's too much secrecy for nothing. Am I terrible?"

"Only a little," I said.

"I just think—there's this girl I know, Addie, who lives in Violet. This isn't the way I thought I would bring it up, but I've kind of wanted to talk to you about this."

My throat constricted. "About what?"

"I was just thinking last night about what if she disappeared, you know? And I saw her name on AwayWeGo and wouldn't know where she went. If we figure out what's going on, we could save her, kid. We could save *everyone*. And I feel that way about you, too. I want to save you. And I want to save Addie. But differently. Do you know what I mean? That's what I realized. I want to save you differently."

I blinked.

"Noah?"

I felt like a wisp of a feather on Pluto.

"Can you not call me kid?" I asked, sharp. A second later, mumbling at my sneakers, both of which stared up bleakly at me: "I don't really understand. Was it Nigel?"

He shook his head. "That's not—that's not it."

He didn't elaborate, so I said, "It's been a long day," which it hadn't been. I'd only been up for eight or so hours. "I think I'm going to bed now."

If I didn't agree, we would still be whatever we were before this conversation. That was how it had to work.

"Noah, I don't want to lose you."

"I think I'm going to bed now."

"Noah?"

"It's been a long day."

He started after me, but stopped himself.

OPINIONS

Action Necessary to Secure Civil Liberties of Youths in Recovery

a society that discriminates against a segment of its population that numbers in the hundred thousands? A segment of the population that has been herded away, shut behind sophisticated, motion-sensing walls, whose communications are monitored and circumscribed, as if this supposedly free nation were the USSR. Why can students receive letters from parents and not phone calls or e-mails? Are a few regrettable incidents just cause for the total infringement of our civil liberties? Westing was pitched to its students as a "one-of-a-kind" institution, devoted to battling for improved conditions for all youths in recovery, but the function it really serves is to give governmental repression a kinder face. The beneficiaries are those students whose high NAAP scores apparently qualify them for a better quality of life than other youths in

Westinger. page 7

FUCKING POLO

For a time Zach and I managed to avoid each other, which was quite impressive, considering we lived in the same hall and saw each other once a week at Polo. We never fully committed ourselves to the effort, though—that way, we had the recourse of plausible deniability if one of us worked up the courage to say, *Hey, what the fuck, man.*

I was watching the year's first snowfall through the window of my twentieth-century lit class when my phone buzzed. I checked it under my desk while my professor lectured about how Cheever's "The Swimmer" is a quest narrative through 1960s American suburbia, as if any of us had any idea of what that meant, really.

can u meet me on the path bw Gall & Caf

Coming I responded.

halfway ;] he said.

So I ditched.

Down the steps of Bullsworth and into the academic quad, filled with brown and golden leaves half hidden by fresh snow. I stepped on a crumpled copy of the *Westinger* strewn on the ground, caught a glance at a headline that read "Director Speaks Out: Westing's Mission to Help, Not Curtail Liberty." A tangle of boys played football, leaves and fresh snow crunching beneath their sneakers.

The football sailed past my head, bounced off Lombardy Hall's brick facade. I headed up past Lombardy, onto the nearest of the cobblestone paths that ran between the cafeteria and Galloway, whipping my phone out, checking to see if Zach had messaged to explain, elaborate, but nothing.

I saw him from afar, on a bench in a small clearing off to the side.

"Hi, Noah," he said, raising his hand in a tentative wave.

"Hi, Zach," I said.

"I wanted to show you something," he said, rising.

"And here I thought you missed me."

He froze momentarily, turned so he stood in profile, brushed a hand through his hair.

"Of course I've missed you. I'm crazy about you, naturally."

"Naturally."

He looked at me, but tentatively, like a scientist who'd just encountered a strange and erratic new species.

"I wanted to show you something. Okay?"

I sighed. "Okay."

He led me into the woods, ducked under a branch, and another, jumped over a stump. He was rushing, leading me—I realized—to one of the traps we'd set with Polo Club. Together with the rest of the club in a conference room on the second floor of the library we'd pored over maps of the neighboring Vermont countryside, discussed which berries and mushrooms were edible, practiced tying knots, making fishing poles and nets and traps.

Dread squirmed inside me, but I couldn't stop now.

I noticed the smell first.

The squirrel was a ruin. Some other animal—badger, maybe—must have gotten at it while it was stuck.

I studied Zach, and he studied me studying him, and I said, "I'm sorry."

He nodded, as if I'd passed some sort of test. The shadows of branches played against his skin as he talked. "You know it's funny. I—when I was a freshman here I found this, umm, wounded rabbit. God, I couldn't get it out of my head. It was a baby. I came back with a box for him. He was upright now, so I reached to touch him, to see if he was okay. I had gloves on, these plastic cleaning things. He almost let me touch him, but then he bolted—didn't get far, sort of flopped on his side." Zach hesitated, bit his lip. He looked self-conscious, like I'd caught him being himself. "God, I don't know why I'm telling you this." He cleared his throat and went on. "I grabbed him and put him in the box and took the box back to my room, set it on my bed. That's when I straight-up panicked. I didn't know what to do with him. I thought he'd die for sure. Didn't know the first thing. So I started petting him, right? Crazy, right? Talking to him. He was in the corner of the box. He let me pet him. He had no fight instinct, Noah. He could've bit me or clawed at me—he had no fight instinct." He threw me a sheepish glance. "Maybe that's what I like about you, kiddo."

My mouth worked, but my brain wasn't cooperating. "What you like," I repeated. A snowflake landed on his brow and melted. The squirrel's guts hung out of its body. Zach frowned at the branches crisscrossing above our heads, as if they were responsible.

He walked this way and that, aimlessly.

I wanted to offer something, but what? A eulogy? What did Zach expect from me? What did he want?

You were a good squirrel, until you got caught up in one of our traps and got disemboweled by a badger. In nomine Patris, et Filii, et Spiritus Sancti, requiescat in pace.

Birds flitted above us in the trees and I wanted to say

something to make things better between us, something romantic and stupid, about how some birds mate for life, but which ones?—my lack of ornithological knowledge was holding me back. You had to know everything about everything, didn't you, in order to say the right thing at the right time, in order to draw the right metaphor out at the right moment and turn that moment into poetry. Maybe that was why the world had poets and playwrights. To give us back all the words we'd squandered.

"I like that I couldn't imagine you hurting someone," Zach said quietly. "Anyone," he amended. "I guess I like that you're not into competition. That you're different. My mom was always drilling into me about sports and grades and being popular, how I was born with every opportunity, so there's absolutely no excuse for being second best. Ra ra no gold medals for second place, Zachary, ra."

I heard, in the distance, the sound of students, teachers, their approaching steps, fragments of conversation punctuated by laughter. Why was he telling me this? We cuddled, he pushed me away, invited me to tea, told me about a girl he liked, and now what? Parental-story-sharing time? Did he not think I could be the best? Did he not think I could protect him?

"I could've beat you in that race," I said. "If we raced now I would beat you."

His mouth worked, but formed no words. The students and teachers had passed. It was quiet again.

"I don't know about that," he said. "I feel terrible and now I'm making you feel terrible. Aren't I?" He massaged his temples, took a couple steps away from me, meandered back. He squinted through the patchwork of trees at something only he could see.

"Is it—are you afraid? I'm afraid, too, Zach."

He shook his head, pressed a hand gently to my shoulder. "That's—that's not it, Noah. Please try to understand. I've missed you, that's all. And I thought you'd understand. I thought I'd bring you here and—I don't know what I thought. I don't know about Addie. We—I spent the night, and then she asked for some space. She said she needed space."

"That sounds familiar, Zach."

He looked pained, but went on. "We just don't have a lot of time. And I don't think I feel that way about you. And maybe she doesn't feel that way about me. That's what's been running through my head. And then I found the squirrel and, *God,* I don't know. I just wanted to save her. I thought if we find out where the sick kids go—"

Ever since I'd started avoiding Zach, I'd made up for it by hanging out with Alice, who was always trying to save me, worrying about my level of alcohol consumption, what I did on Friday nights.

"Maybe she doesn't want to be saved," I said. "Why do you need to save her?"

"Everyone wants to be saved, kid," he said in surprise. "It's just a question of who's doing the saving."

His hand dangled at his side. I could reach out and hold it. I could push him against a tree and kiss him, or punch him. I took a step toward him, and he tensed. That killed me, so I stopped.

"Noah," he said.

"We—" *Cuddled* was the next word I had in mind, but it sounded ridiculous. Unable to capture what I mean. Unable to capture the closeness of two people. "That night. We *raced*."

"It was fun," he admitted.

"We could just have fun," I said, trying not to beg. "It wouldn't have to be anything. Just fun."

He shook his head, sad. "It's not a good idea, Noah."

That's when I heard the sound of an engine making its way along the forest path. Zach squinted through the trees at the source of the sound, and when he made out the construction truck, a change came over him.

"Noah," he said. "Don't you wonder where those trucks go?"

OPINIONS

Director Speaks Out: Westing's Mission to Help, Not Curtail Liberty

those among you who complain of the infringement of rights. But the Internet is filled with a proliferation of insensitive material, and in the past, when Internet access was unrestricted, cyber-bullies targeted recovering youths. As for contact with parents, do students remember when parental contact was left unchecked? Do students desire a repeat of Houston? At any other high school in America, many students here would have hanging over them the very real probability of expulsion. Yet Westing has only ever expelled those found guilty of committing sexual and/or violent offenses. We have been lenient and liberal in our policies, transparent about hospice care in the tertiary clinics and next steps in the recovery process Restrictions are in place for the protection of students

Westinger. Page 2

SEVEN WEEKS
BEFORE THE
CATACLYSMIC,
FIERY, KIND OF
CLICHÉD END
OF ALL THINGS
(OR NoT)

BLESS YOU

I wake.

Through the window, I watch a construction truck roll along a path leading to the northeast section of the wall. The construction workers have been working at the wall all month, but nobody ventures close enough to see why.

Beside me, Alice is asleep again, her chest rising and falling, contentment written on her face. Garbage duty really takes it out of you. I brush a hand through her hair. So many gray strands. One, two, three . . . The meds fuck everyone up differently. Seven, eight, nine. . . I get to twenty-three grays until I can't take it anymore, so I roll out of Alice's bed, leaving her to frequent whatever happy places there are to be found in the crevices of her mind.

The Polo key is still in my hand. I slip it into my mouth again.

My computer waits on the kitchen table, by a bowl of unfinished cereal that's gone untouched for several days. Whatever milk was once there has probably turned to yogurt. AwayWeGo calls to me—I try to resist, fail—while I wait for a plateful of hot dogs and bland potatoes to be sufficiently nuked so as to approach edibility, only to realize I don't want to go through the effort of chewing. Marty's probably still out Russian-ing it up in the library. I *could* send him some annoying texts of the *Are you jacking off to Turgenev again?* variety. Again. I could, but shouldn't, so I do.

He gives me the silent treatment.

I spit the key out onto a paper napkin, get up, and excavate a bottle of vodka from inside a box of Capt'n Crunch labeled Noah Falls. Alice is sleeping and happy, and I, too, want some of this happiness business I keep hearing so much about. Unlike Alice, I rarely find fulfillment in my dreams, though once I dreamed of Zach and me walking through some nameless gray city, holding hands. No, it didn't turn into a wet dream. Not this one, at least. All we did was hold hands; in the dream I did not have leprosy, did not have to moisturize five times a day.

I pour myself half a cup of the vodka, drop in a couple ice cubes, sniff, and wince.

I'll never understand why Marty and Alice do what they do. What good is all that work when you'll probably go away long before you finish your footnotes, have your name listed on AwayWeGo alongside your already departed friends and peers, right beside this month's list of Age of Rome's high scores?

Speaking of Age of Rome, I load the game up to distract myself from the mediocrity of my dinner.

No, Age of Rome, I don't want you to challenge my AwayWeGo friends to beat my campaign score.

No, Age of Rome, I don't want you to post my battle results to my AwayWeGo profile.

No, Age of Rome, I don't want to give you my Social Security number.

By the time Marty stumbles back to the apartment, I have Jerusalem under siege and I'm in quite good spirits, but I've barely touched my food. I tried to buy Jerusalem. When that didn't work, I sent my trusted General Flavius Something-or-other to sort the bastards out. Noble Flavius died on the way to the Holy Land. His son Decimus has taken the father's place and seems the capable sort, judging by the one-square-inch picture of him in the corner of my screen.

"Marty-guy!"

"Oh," he says from the foyer. "Hello, Noah." Always so formal, Martin, with his hellos and good-byes. You'll never get a "see ya later, alligator" out of him, tell you that much.

"Come 'ere, I need your help."

He surveys my screen with a slight frown.

"Egypt's got a couple armies closing in on you—"

"We're not at war with Egypt, though. Egypt and I are bros."

"And they've got a navy right near your harbor."

"I'm not at war with Egypt, though," I say. "I just paid them fifty thousand florins the other turn . . . Fifty thousand florins, Martin. Fifty thousand florins don't grow on trees."

That's when he notices my bottle of vodka.

He shakes his head, smiling reluctantly. "Should've known."

"You and me, Marty-guy. Two sides of the same coin. Like, you're heads and I'm tails. Together we're worth twenty-five cents."

"Noah."

"What?"

"Screen."

I turn my attention back to the screen. My virtual enemies are pouring out of the gates of Jerusalem in hopes of catching me by surprise and—*largely*—succeeding. I throw Marty a death glare.

He shrugs. "I tried to warn you—"

A half hour and two shots later, I have a Pyrrhic victory on my hands. Jerusalem is mine, but the great legion that Rome sent forth is largely gone. Within three turns, Jerusalem falls to Egypt, Egyptian navies blockade my ports, and the accursed

Gauls, whose forces I never quite finished off, descend on me from the north in my moment of weakness.

I enlist mercenaries who turn on me.

I build ships that cannot breach the Egyptian blockades.

I send out diplomats who are turned away.

The fate of my empire appears increasingly bleak, so I drink increasing amounts of vodka to compensate, until it increasingly occurs to me that Marty-guy's sobriety is an unacceptable state of affairs that must be rectified with all due haste.

"Hey Marty-guy," I say, cupping a hand to my ear. "You hear that?"

"Huh?"

"That's the sound of one guy. Drinking alone."

He undergoes a very brief internal struggle, because he cares that Alice doesn't like drinking. "Okay," he says.

"Alice is sleeping," I point out, as if this should assuage any possible guilt.

I pour him a shot.

Just then, as the combined might of the Gauls, the Parthians, the Egyptians, and the Carthaginians storm the gates of my Rome, I get a pop-up message:

CONGRATULATIONS NOAH FALLS
SARAH AND JACOB FALLS HAVE TRIBUTED YOU
10,000 AGE OF ROME FLORINS.
SEND A THANK-YOU CARD
TO THEIR MAILING ADDRESS FOR ONLY $7.99?

Mom's voice, her laugh, that red door, how hot the metal knob got on stifling summer days. A diorama we once made together for school. It had something to do with a giraffe.

Should I buy her a thank-you card with her own money? Is a giraffe diorama worth $7.99 and a son's discomfort?

"It's not just Alice, though," he says, and I know he means our parents. What would they think of us? Marty worries about stuff like that.

As for me, I X out the pop-up immediately and don't speak for a time. I do nothing as my Rome is sacked and burned, and a part of me wants to cry, for all those imaginary empires we work so hard to build on the backs of virtual slaves and micro-transactions, gifts from parents we last saw when we were nine, empires that in the end must succumb to the eternal return of the game-over screen, until Marty gently pries the shot I poured for him out of my fingers and downs it with admirable form.

This is his apology for bringing up the parents.

He's the best, like that.

He coughs, throws me a look of reproach, coughs again. *Christ*, Noah."

"You need to drink more," I say. "Like Tolstoy, it gets better the more you put into it."

"I can't believe you just compared—"

"Believe it, Marty-guy. Believe it."

I try to sound cheery. There's no point in being sad. But every couple weeks, my parents send me Age of Rome florins or Pirate World booty and that kills me. They even donated an extra shipment of Growth Hormone to my Factoryfarmville factory farm the other day. Why do they keep sending me these things, when I never send them anything in return? When I never open their letters?

Marty watches me pour him a second shot. I spill a bit of vodka on the table. "Here," I say, handing him the shot glass. He toasts me, but his eyes are sad.

"Close your eyes, please," I say, and the wonderful thing about being drunk together is that he listens without so much as raising a question. I wipe away my tears and we go out to have an adventure, because there's something about having a BAC above .15 that makes everything possible, including but not limited to acute alcohol poisoning. We take my vodka with us, of course, passing it back and forth. Security patrols clack by in their hard plastic boots. They won't bother us unless we get too close to the lamp-lit walls. We cut through the residential quad until we reach the lawn in front of Galloway, the parking lot empty save for a handful of cars, overnight workers at the Wellness Center, probably—there's a figure standing at a window on the third floor, the floor that girls at Westing sometimes go up to, and for two weeks afterward aren't supposed to take baths or have sex or use tampons.

Marty takes another gulp of vodka.

He's caught up with me enough that it doesn't matter he's not caught up with me. He gazes up at the stars transfixed, and I think of Whitman's learn'd astronomer, a dissident student fleeing the lecture hall, fleeing a reduction of the world to equations and formulas, and instead, looking up in perfect silence at the stars. Alice wanted to teach me the constellations, but I told her all I saw were a whole lot of balls of fire. Which of us was right? Are the stars mythic Greek figures, or simply a bunch of hot air? Are we atoms, or do we have souls? If you don't know which story is right, then how is it possible to know whether you should be sitting in the lecture hall or standing outside with your head tilted skyward, praying in Church or huddled over a physics problem set?

I ask these questions of Marty, and his response is "What?" Impressively, he manages to slur the one syllable.

"What do you mean, 'what'?"

"I mean—what do *you* mean?"

"Well, which part didn't you get? The Whitman reference? That was very Westing of me, wasn't it? There's also an implied part, but I'm not sure what I implied."

"It's like you're talking Japanese. Never mind."

"So I'm talking English?"

"No. Yes. I mean—you're talking Japanese. I just don't want to offend the Japanese. I have a Japanese friend, you know."

"But, Marty," I say, "if I'm talking Japanese, then how do you understand me enough to know you're not understanding me?"

"I'm, uh, taking an intro class."

That explains absolutely everything. For a few minutes neither of us speaks, until, I don't quite know why, but I tell him, "I miss your play."

I haven't acted in a while. Sometimes I think it's for the best—I act plenty as Noah, no need to take on other personas when I have my hands so full with this one. But during the spring, in Marty's take on *Peter Pan*, I became the boy who would never grow old. The play took place in a quarantine ward in an unnamed children's hospital. There was a corridor with two entrances, a door on the right and a door on the left. Doctors entered in the morning and exited in the evening through the door on the right, which was guarded by soldiers, soldiers with guns. Sick children were wheeled out in stretchers through the door on the left. The doctors would return with empty stretchers. Peter and Wendy, like all the children on the ward, were afflicted with an unspecified disease, but whenever they got scared, about their disappearing friends, about the world outside, which magazines from a magazine rack reported was full of things like the Iranian Nuclear Program and the unlikelihood of Europe meeting its climate goals, they read *Game Informer* instead, and when *Game Informer* wasn't enough, they escaped to Neverland by drawing a blanket over themselves at precisely 2:33 in the morning and sharing Skittles. The Skittles were the key, the incantation, Neverland was impossible without them. Once in Neverland, they could play all the games that *Game Informer* talked about, months before their release dates.

"Do you think Alice liked it?" he asks.

The question takes me by surprise. I respond automatically, but gain confidence as the words spill out of my mouth. "Of course she did. Anyone with half a brain liked it. More than liked it. And Alice has two halves of a brain. One full brain, Marty-guy. She was all over it."

Marty looks like he wants to say something, but before he can, he erupts into a coughing fit, stumbles over to a nearby bench.

"Bless you," I say, ridiculously.

"I'm energy, you know," Marty says. "So much energy. The Buddhists say that I have the universe in the tip of my finger, in case you were wondering, and Tolstoy says religion is our relation to the infinite world." To clarify, he adds, "Tolstoy wasn't a Buddhist."

"Which finger?" I drop into the seat next to him.

"What?"

"Which finger is it that you have a universe in? I mean it's definitely not your pinky." I take his hand in mine to illustrate my point. "Your pinky is—it's too small Marty. It's unrealistic to think. Now, your index finger maybe, *maybe*, but your pinky—"

"The universe was smaller than my pinky," he protests. "Right after the big bang. Right after the big bang, it was so small a million universes could've fit into my pinky. Not to mention my index finger."

"It's a damn fine index finger," I say. "For fitting universes in . . . I just wish those fingers would write another play."

"There's no point," he says despondently. His glasses have fallen askew. "I didn't want to write a play, anyway. I wanted to write something holy. About parents and walls and killer comets. I wanted to make someone love me. Do you think you can write something to make someone love you?"

"I don't know," I say quietly.

"I wanted to *see* them. . . The way people look at you when they love you—nobody's ever looked at me that way, so I wanted to see—" He doesn't finish, but he doesn't have to. Every week at checkups, Marty stares at the eye chart and hopes it hasn't gotten blurrier. For now, the meds help, but he is afraid of when they won't.

"You said before—here's the point, Marty. A story is your chance for things to make sense."

"Noah?" he says.

"Yeah?"

"Can I have a hug?"

That kills me.

I reach out, and hug him, and he hugs me back.

Act 1: Scene 3

[*Peter and Wendy are perusing magazines in Peter's room. They are scared by the magazines that discuss current affairs. Peter picks up the latest edition of* Game Informer, *flips through it. They ignore the guards outside in the corridor, the children being wheeled out, the empty stretchers.*]

> **PETER**
> The thing is, I don't understand sports games. You have a choice between saving the universe from an alien race bent on the total annihilation of all sentient life but choose to shoot a ball through a hoop instead?

> **WENDY**
> [*shrugging*]:
> Boys have a hero complex.

> **PETER**
> Oh yeah? And what about girls, then?

> **WENDY**
> Girls have been socialized by millennia of patriarchal oppression to accept how disappointing reality is. We know not to expect more from a world run by men. We know not to

expect to be heroes. Shooting a
ball through a hoop is like icing
on the cake. Of gender oppression.

                    PETER
[*casts a meaningful look at Wendy*]:
I thought we liked games because we
didn't have to talk about this shit.

                    WENDY
I like games because, in those
moments when I can get around the
stylized depiction of a woman's
form, by which I mean boobs so
big they have boys locked into
gravitational orbit around them—

                    PETER
You say that like it's a bad thing.

                    WENDY
I sometimes feel like a kid again.
With my brother, I used to play
this game where we would hide
under the blanket and pretend we
were space explorers, or pilots of
armored suits.

                    PETER
                [hesitant]:
Want to try?

THERE'S NO PLACE LIKE HOME

It takes Marty and me a few minutes of fumbling before we work the door open and stumble back into the apartment, Marty going on about something Tolstoy once said. In the kitchen, I pour us a glass of water each. My largely untouched plate of hot dogs and potatoes glares at me with accusation. Marty collapses at the kitchen table.

He squints at something to the right of my plate, picks up the key I left on the table. "Is *this*—this is the one we stole."

"It was in my mouth," I confess.

"Oh." He frowns in concentration. "I keep my keys in my wallet, because—" He breaks off mid-sentence to rush for the bathroom, dropping the key with a clack. I laugh. What a lightweight. I follow, bringing his glass of water with me. He's hunched over the toilet. He lifts his head up long enough to give me a scathing look, before turning back to the pressing matter of throwing up his dinner.

"Better?"

His response is to retch more. Once I'm pretty sure he's done, I try again. "Better?"

"Yeah." He gets up, a little unsteadily, and rinses out his mouth. I hand him his glass of water.

"Noah—"

"Drink. You'll want to kiss me thank you in the morning."

He hands the glass back to me when he's done with a *Happy now?* sort of gesture. I walk him up the stairs to his room, set a trash can by his bed. I can't help noticing there's a crumpled old F.L.Y. newsletter inside.

"Peter. Hey—hey—" Marty grabs my arm. "Can you tell Wendy—can you tell her—" His voice trails off.

"What, buddy?"

But he grows confused, closes his eyes. "Tell her—"

He doesn't finish the thought.

In my room, I strip down to my underwear, leaving my clothes strewn across the floor. Sometime in the night, I will wake, I will reach for my phone, I will dial my old house number, and press the cell to my ear, and listen for the sound of Mom's voice, prepared to thank her for her florins.

I will hear: "Welcome to AwayWeCall Wireless. We are sorry, but your number cannot be completed as dialed. Please check the number and dial again."

AGE OF ROME
‹ THE DEFENSE OF ROME ›

BATTLE RESULTS—**CATACLYSMIC** DEFEAT

MEN DEPLOYED | KILLS | MEN REMAINING

	MEN DEPLOYED	KILLS	MEN REMAINING
YOUR ARMY (ROME)	12	-1	O
ENEMY ARMY (GAUL)	1762	10	1762
ENEMY ARMY (EGYPT)	698	1	689
ENEMY ARMY (PARTHIA)	212	O	212
ENEMY ARMY (CARTHAGE)	142	O	142

ALLOW AGE OF ROME TO POST BATTLE RESULTS TO YOUR PROFILE?
   [YES]   [**NO**]

DREAMS OF HOME

Noah is a boy made of raindrops.

He reaches inside himself, and picks one raindrop out.

It looks like this: o

Inside the raindrop are shadows lingering in a familiar doorway late at night. But the raindrop is small and slippery. It falls through his fingers, so he reaches inside himself again, and picks out a second raindrop.

It looks like this: o

Inside the raindrop is the creak of floorboards under the weight of woolen slippers.

Again, the raindrop slips away.

Again, he reaches inside himself.

With more droplets come more visions.

o: A soft voice that recounts fairy tales—"Three Little Pigs," "Cinderella," and so on.

o: Fingers callused from years of gardening work, callused but warm.

o: A beard going gray.

o: Lipstick the color of fire, a kiss the color of fire, on a cheek flushed pink with winter and embarrassment.

o: The tide of the ocean on summer days, rising and receding with the laughter of beautiful not-quite-adults playing volleyball on a long-ago holiday.

o: The feel of hair being tousled by—*brother*?

o: Dry turkey and canned cranberry sauce on Thanksgiving Day, giving thanks to God for family.

o: His older brother was Jonathan?—until Jonathan got sick, went away. His mother is still Sarah and his father is still Jacob. They will still be Sarah and Jacob, Jacob and Sarah, though maybe not Sarah and Jacob together, on the hour and the minute and the second that not-Jonathan and not-Noah are reunited, the hour and the minute and the second when they are not on a beach again, with the tide and the teenagers playing volleyball, and Jonathan doesn't reach over to stroke his brother's hair, the summer before college, doesn't cough, doesn't pull his hand away to cover his mouth, doesn't say, through teary eyes, "Damn."

o: A reflection of a nine-year-old boy left behind in the mirror of a second-floor bathroom in a nineteenth-century colonial. A real mirror, in a real bathroom, in a real house, far beyond the walls of Westing.

Droplet by droplet, let Noah forget the shadows and the lipstick, the summer holidays and ever believing in God. Let Noah forget Noah. The reflections he leaves behind are more real than he is, anyway. He is never more present than to those for whom he is absent.

So let Noah empty himself, little by little. It is whispered that the virus attacks the brain last, the memories last. There are rumors that memories are downloaded onto chips and sold to adults who want to remember their first loves and homework handed in two minutes before a deadline.

It would be terrible if the rumors were true and terrible if they weren't.

But Noah still has some raindrops left inside himself.

He holds the remaining drops in a pool in his hand, and for now, they do not slip through his fingers.

In the pool, he sees himself waking up with a raging hangover, his seventeenth birthday six days away. Nobody at Westing publicizes or celebrates their birthday.

THE DIFFERENCE BETWEEN BAD LIARS AND GOOD PEOPLE

It isn't even dawn yet, but I am already waiting for the day to be over.

I can never seem to have both a good night of drinking and a good night of sleep. Always have to choose between the two, and my priorities have accustomed me to this pre-morning quiet, where I sit picking at my chapped lips, the dried, cracked skin on my forearms. Through the blinds on the kitchen window—a familiar sight—the sun rises over the lake, the sky turns orange, our twig of an apple tree leans precariously. I am too tired to care about the beauty of such things. I light a cigarette to keep me company while time passes, until someone descends from on high to go to the bathroom, and in one magnificent toilet flush, brings the world into being.

I exhale, the smoke curls, and I'm taken back to the curl of smoke on the porch of a house the moment before it disperses into the air of a distant summer, a house without a wall, without so much as a fence, a father cloaked in shadow, features indistinguishable, but his voice is gruff, harsh, it scares me and yet I do not want to stop listening to it, he is telling me something, he is telling me about his work, I am too young to understand, the smell of pie drifts through the open window, and Dad is telling me he stays late at work to finish graduate school assignments, he is telling me his boss comes into the office to check up on him at 7 p.m. smelling of alcohol, harasses him for doing homework at the workplace. I try to pick the memory apart. I suspect it's a dream. The only way to know would be to answer my parents' letters, to call and ask.

Fifteen minutes to seven—footsteps on the stairs. Alice peeks into the kitchen, her hair disheveled. She scrunches her nose at my cigarette, but says nothing. It is too early for argument. We sit together, sipping coffee at the table. She sets her cup down with a soft clack and leans in toward me. She kisses me on the neck, soft. Into my ear, she says, "I missed you last night. I don't sleep well when you're not there. Did you know that?"

"I, on the other hand, sleep better. You always hog the pillows. And kick me when I pry one from you. I swear, when you're asleep I see a whole 'nother side to you."

She nudges me with her elbow. "'Hog' is a strong word. I prefer 'take into protective custody.'"

"Well we need to hash out a better joint-custody agreement."

"I prefer the current arrangement," she says.

"You would."

She kisses my ear, my throat. "Come to bed with me?"

I laugh.

"I'm serious," she says, bumping my shoulder playfully with hers. "Let's spend the morning in bed. We can plan next week's picnic. I know how much you're looking forward to it." She smiles a sad smile. "But please finish that *thing*"—she prefers not to dignify the cigarette by referring to it by name—"before you come up."

"You want to stay in bed and skip chapel services? That's not like you."

"It's a *Saturday*, silly goose," she says.

This silly goose finishes his cigarette, lets Alice lead him upstairs, where she pretends not to care about the lingering smell of ash.

I like the smell, but I wouldn't know how to explain why. Dad on the porch, Alex and me in the library beside a urinal. Commemorating these things would be worth the cancer even if I was outside the walls, if no one was going to come and take me away.

She unbuttons her gown. Takes my shirt off. Next my pants. My underwear. She pushes me down, onto the bed, her palms cold against my skin. I feel her lips, her hot breath, on my stomach, my belly button, my groin. . .

"Close your eyes," she says.

"You're sure? You don't usually—"

"Please close your eyes."

I close my eyes and moan quietly. I don't want her to stop, but I force myself to say, "Are you—" I leave the thought hanging. When she doesn't answer, I don't ask again.

When she's done, I do her. Then I roll out of the bed and say, "Don't move a goddamn inch."

She moves her toe a goddamn inch, her eyes twinkling mischievously.

Downstairs I make blueberry pancakes, because Alice and her grandma would eat them on summer evenings, out on the porch. Grandma would sprinkle sugar on top. It would go dark and her grandma would teach her the constellations, Big Dippers and Little Dippers. Her grandma writes sometimes, and Alice writes back, of course she does; they reminisce about celestial silverware.

I kick open the door to Alice's room, struggling with the tray of food. Pancakes, jam, scrambled eggs, two glasses of milk. Three steps into the room I catch my foot on a pair of Alice's shoes and everything that comes up must go down. I want to jest, to make light of the situation.

Instead, I begin to cry. She made these sucking noises, and I let her make them, the girl whose grandma taught her the constellations, the same constellations I told her I was uninterested in, and there is the lingering taste of her in my mouth. I tasted Alex, once. He tasted better—like salty-sweet potato chips. The truth is I didn't like returning the favor for Alice; the truth is it made my neck hurt.

She hugs me, I get a whiff of her strawberry shampoo, and I feel nauseous. She must've taken a shower while I was preparing this—*mess*.

"Why did you—" I hesitate, can't get the words out. I look at Alice—Alice, who believes, who read an article on AwayWeGo about Coca Cola's alleged anti-union activities in Latin America and now wants to kick it off campus, she wants to save Latin American union workers, and she wants to save me, too, to have me counseled into happiness. I taste vomit in the back of my throat as we clean up the floor together.

"Noah?" she asks as I throw a wet paper towel in the trash and head for the door to grab another roll.

"If I'd known this would happen, I'd have made sandwiches," I say, wiping at my eye with my arm.

"You still can," she says, missing my joke. "When we do our picnic. If you can suspend your nothing-matters-everything-is-futile—"

"A tall order," I say, to humor her.

"—you might actually have fun! I promise you will."

I'm waiting for her to tell me that talking to someone about my feelings would help. To tell me that crying over a spilled breakfast is. Not. Normal.

"Love you," is what she says. Her eyes flick away from my face.

"Love you, too," I mumble back, and my heart cramps up. Good liars have stone hearts. I don't have a stone heart, but that doesn't make me a good person.

It does, however, make me a bad liar.

"Noah," she says, her voice hesitant. "It's coming up, isn't it? It's very soon now?"

She means my birthday.

"Yes," I admit. "Soon."

Kick Coke

I can still drink Pepsi though right?

In light of Coca Cola's history of human rights violations, we, the undersigned, are resolved to demand an immediate end to Westing's affiliation with Coca Cola. It is our duty, as citizens of a global community, to act in a manner that is commensurate with the well-being of all people, within our walls and outside fo them, in America and abroad.

Alice Witaker	Jenna Fairbanks	Alberta Figueroa
Neil G. Phelps	Alyssa Meyers	Yen-Chiao Huang
Cindy Corval	Joshua Lesters	Toby Fell-Holsten
Alexa Ban Hauten	Hanna Silverstein	Rachel Coen
Ivan Weatherby	Kyle Kraus	Noah Falls
Sue Xing	Michael Long	Maria Fernandez
Daniel Faustern	Michael Studebaker	Yana Ostov
Nick Greenblatt	Shane Atkinson	Ephraim Kossavy
Tory Irving	Luigi Perelli	Rashad Jennings
Nick Chu	Jie Chen	

Feeling
L O W ?

Warning Signs of Depression Include:

- ✗ Feelings of Hopelessness
- ✗ Thoughts of Suicide
- ✗ Mood Swings
- ✗ Loss of Appetite
- ✗ Fatigue
- ✗ Irregular Sleep

The **Westing Counseling Service** Is Here to Help

Change Your into a

Make an Appointment **TODAY**

Wellness Center, 2nd Floor*801-20-16

NOAH V. THE GREAT TRAGIC POWERS OF THE WORLD

We're out picnicking by the lake, on a day so beautiful you can't help feeling as miserable as if you had just turned seventeen, which, in fact, I have.

I think Marty and Alice have figured it out, but they know better than to congratulate me on my increased proximity to death.

I am commemorating the occasion by juggling.

Learning to juggle is the one incontrovertible way I've managed to better myself in the year since I came to Westing, because what else is a lonely, sexually frustrated boy to do but to get his hands on as many balls as possible? Or in today's case, *apples*. The apples rise and fall and rise and fall as Alice talks about the newsies.

"—it's just so important that they know about all the resources the campus has to offer. Westing counseling"—she shoots me a meaningful look—"the sexual assault hotline, the office of residential life. I know personally how hard the adjustment can be."

Marty's nodding, maintaining eye contact, almost as if he cares, while the two of them feign interest in my display of manual dexterity. I'm about to make a comment like *I doubt a shrink could counsel meaning into life*, but Alice knows me too well. "You look like you're in the mood to argue," she says, studying me with a small frown.

"You would know, seeing as we do it so much. What do they say? Ten thousand hours of practice leads to mastery?"

I catch the apples, spill them into the blanket between us.

"We don't do it *that* much," she says.

I glance at Marty for support. He gives me his patented deer-in-the-headlights look.

"More than a little but less than a lot?" he offers, and stuffs his face with a sandwich to avoid further questioning.

"The other day we argued about my socks. Remember that?" I say as I turn back to Alice.

"Well, they were on the communal sofa and I thought—"

"It was one sock, Alice. One lonely, little sock, somehow accidentally—" I stop myself. "See? See? We almost started arguing about arguing about socks."

"The truth is, *I* went to counseling, Noah," Alice says. She has a way of stating simple facts that feels like chastisement. "I know it may be hard for you to imagine, but it helps. They teach you strategies to reframe your thinking."

"About dying?"

"About living." She bites her lip. "You barely even eat. I worry."

My turn to sigh. "I was working up to it, you know. Arguing, I mean. But you ruined it."

"I know," she says.

I love that she knows, so I lean over and give her a brief kiss. For once, my thoughts do not drift to Zach.

Marty cracks open some Pushkin, pretends to read *Eugene Onegin*. He does an admirable job, even goes as far as to mouth the words.

"Martin, dear?" I say.

Marty looks up, and I say, "If Pushkin is the best Russians

can do," I say, "they ought to stick to chess, balalaika, and scorched earth tactics."

"Noah," he says. Shakes his head. "I don't even know where to start."

"You can start by dropping that," I say, nodding at his book.

"Have you even read Pushkin?"

"As a matter of fact I have. Dr. Seuss can write better limericks, frankly."

He gives me such a helplessly exasperated look that I feel guilty. I'm about to apologize when Alice says, "Noah Falls. You're such a troll."

I want to tell them I was perfectly serious; the other week I spent a good hour crying over *Oh, the Places You'll Go!*

"It's okay," Marty says. "Noah has this thing where he has to annoy me periodically. And get me drunk."

"And look out for you after he's gotten you drunk," I say, forcing brightness into my voice.

"And look out for me after he's gotten me drunk."

Alice smiles wistfully at Marty. "You're too good to him, you know?"

Marty blushes, turns a page, but Alice has turned her attention to me. Doubt flickers over her face. She thinks she's hurt my feelings, and now she's about to apologize. I hate how fragile she thinks I am; she doesn't understand that I'm the one who's hurting her. It strikes me that the only functional relationship I've ever had was in Marty's *Peter Pan*. Peter's vision was failing, Wendy's hair was turning gray, but it was okay, because they were in love, and every night they would escape to Neverland together.

"Noah?" Alice asks, and her voice jolts me from my thoughts.

Marty hunches over *Eugene Onegin*, adjusts his glasses.

"You're right, actually," I say, and suddenly I'm standing. Marty and Alice stare up at me from the ground, perplexed.

They are both too good to me.

And no matter how good they are to me, it's not enough.

Why can't it be enough?

Why do I have to walk around with a nagging emptiness inside me?

"Noah," Alice says, quiet. "You're the best person I know. I believe that."

"I'm—" *Terrible* is the next word I have in mind. Briefly I'm back on the cobblestone path with the autumn-bare branches overhead, the birds flitting above, the teachers approaching, and Zach's telling me he's terrible and I'm thinking of squandered poetry, birds that mate for life.

"—going for a walk" is how I finish. I start down the path that circles the lake, leaving Marty and Alice to stare after me. The Galloway gardens are up ahead, flowers wilting from the heat, the water in the fountain dappled in the light. I shoulder through the back entrance of Galloway, past students sipping coffee and eating goddamn sandwiches in the Academy Café, down a corridor and then another, past the elevator bank, into the lobby.

I don't know where I'm going.

I don't know where I'm going.

I have nowhere to go.

So I stand in the middle of the lobby like the statue of a lost boy.

Counseling, she keeps bringing up counseling.

Sure, there are times when the emptiness is too much, when all I want to do is sleep, or drink. Times when beauty is unbearable. Times when I am in bed with Alice and it seems like

I will be in bed with her forever, and I feel forever like a weight on my chest. But these feelings are a manifestation of and a communion with what Foucault calls the great tragic powers of the world, and I don't want to be medicated out of them. I live on a rock hurtling around a giant ball of fire suspended in a void of infinite nothingness. The only way to transcend that nothingness is through *art, love, work, play, religion,* what else is there? But transcendence is impossible, it's a fanciful tale; what is empty can carry no weight. If I ever forget that fact, the great tragic powers of the world remind me of how little I am, how small I am, because as students stream by me, in and out of the lobby doors, I catch intermittent glances of Westing's walls.

I decide to spend my birthday with the one person I know who doesn't want to be with me, but I hesitate, pacing back and forth outside Clover House's multipurpose room.

This is where I bump into Addie. We know each other the way strangers on a small campus know each other—through distant silhouettes, the flash of a passing face, and AwayWeGo status updates. She takes me in with big brown eyes and says, "Oh. I'm glad—he'll be happy to see a friend."

Friend. The word echoes in my head as she disappears around a corner, leaving me alone with her label. Now I can't change my mind, can't do what I do best and run away, because she'll ask Zach tomorrow if I came and he'll say no I didn't; that's not behavior worthy of a *friend.*

At his door, I knock.

He doesn't answer.

I let my breath out; didn't realize I was holding it.

I knock a second time, loud, clear. He says, "Come in."

I edge the door open.

He smiles from his bed. "Oh, man. Long time no see."

He's lost weight, but he's still beautiful. I can think of no other way to describe him. Too pretty to die, because, of course, the right to life increases in direct proportion to facial symmetry, as judged by your friendly seventeen-year-old arbiter of life and death.

"Distance makes the heart grow fonder, so I spent the last week or so in Alaska," I explain.

His face is inscrutable for a beat, but he breaks into a laugh. "Oh yeah? How'd that go?"

"I wrestled a bear," I say as I slide a chair over to the bedside and take a seat.

"Hey, wouldn't you know? That's what I was about to guess!"

"The bear won."

His hand is inches from mine.

"You and I, kid, we don't believe in competition, though," Zach says. "Oh I know, I know, I know we live in a world where everyone is like ra ra ra fight to the death—"

"What was that?" I said, cupping a hand to my ear. "I didn't catch that."

"Ra ra ra fight to the death," he repeated, "But we, you and me kid, we defy the paradigm that delineates bear wrestling into a win/lose binary in which man must either prevail or be prevailed over by bear."

"Speak for yourself. I wanted the bear to eat my dust."

I could take his hand. It's right there, atop the blanket.

"I believe that's a racing metaphor. Not suited to bear wrestling."

"Name me a bear-wrestling metaphor," I say.

"I can't." He throws both hands up in exasperation.

"Also, if you're racing, and you use a racing metaphor, it's not a metaphor then, is it? It's literal. So bear wrestling might be a perfectly appropriate time to use a racing metaphor and a race might be a perfectly appropriate time to use a bear-wrestling metaphor, because if there's one thing we want to preserve, it's the metaphor-literality binary."

"But kiddo," Zach says, delighted, "bear-wrestling metaphors, they don't exist! Nobody wrestles bears! It's a myth propagated by outdoorsmen who need to bolster their fragile sense of masculinity while traipsing around in fabulously bright clothes—"

"Zach," I say, because this is too much. I like banter. It's light and airy, induces weightlessness without the need for leaving Earth's atmosphere, tons of rocket fuel. But too much of it, and you feel diffuse enough to disappear the moment you step through the door. The only thing grounding me is this knot that has formed in my chest.

"—and sleeping in tents with other men," he finishes.

The knot tightens. "Zach," I say. "It's my birthday."

His face goes rigid, his blue eyes sad. "It's terrible, isn't it?" he says finally. "A terrible day. I'm sorry."

He takes my hand, gives it a squeeze. His is warm and clammy and wonderful.

I could ask him to drink with me, birthday shots. When I drink the pretenses fall away. The more I drink, the less I have to act. Could Zach be acting, too? He must be acting—I want so much to see him as he really is, to make up for volumes of lost poetry. And speaking of paradigms, if Zach succumbs to that drunken urge, so common to Westing, to subvert the clothes-body paradigm, well, that's a price I'm willing to pay.

"Do you want to drink tonight?"

He retracts his hand by pretending to scratch an itch on his nose.

"I don't know if that's a good idea." He says it so gently I can barely hear him. "I mean I'd love to, Addie's got me cooped up in here, it's like house arrest, I tell you. 'Zachary, the doctor told you not to get up unnecessarily'; 'Zachary, the doctor told you to drink more water'; 'Zachary, no junk food'; Zachary Zachary Zachary. She won't even let me have *candy*. Too much sugar. God, I tell you, kid, I've never been more annoyed with the sound of my own name. But I don't know if it's a good idea."

I don't want a clarification of their on-and-off-again status. I don't want to know, I don't want to know. . . .

"Are you guys—" I start, change my mind. "I was thinking— about the day we ran in the rain. Remember?"

He gives me a wan smile, but his eyes focus on his bedsheets. He pushes himself up against the headboard of his bed and says "Not really." The knot in my chest pulls at every muscle in my body.

He keeps talking, but I'm not really listening. Why did I come here? He has this impossible capacity for vacillation, for making me as confused as he is, except maybe he's not confused at all. If I mean nothing to him, then the world will go on without me easily. It will simply spin merrily along. I want someone somewhere to throw a fit, punch a wall, rail against the great tragic powers of the world.

"You don't remember letting me win?"

"So you admit I was beating you?" he says.

"You don't remember my head in your lap?"

"No," he says quietly.

"You don't remember lying in bed together?"

"I'm sorry," he says.

I wipe my brow, which is sticky with sweat from an afternoon by the lake. Alice told me I was the best.

"I think you're the best," I tell him.

He cringes at that, but I continue: "Do you ever think about—giving it a try? Us?"

He shakes his head. "I'm sorry, Noah," he mumbles under his breath.

I pitch forward, my head in my hands, and don't move for fear he'll see me crying. The bed screeches, and I feel his hand in my hair.

I look up at him, and he stares back at me with a stricken expression and says, "God."

There are no clean dishes in our apartment.

The stack of dirties rises past the ledge of the sink, so I set about doing what must be done while a light rain begins to knock against the roof. Several times the drain clogs with food, and several times I clean it out with my fingers.

"Hi, Noah." Alice's voice makes me jump. She's where the door would be, if our kitchen had a door, a door I could lock. She watches me intently as I dry a cup, her drenched hair glossy in the light.

"It's fascinating stuff, I know," I say.

"Noah Falls, you know better than this. You shouldn't be doing this, not on your—" she stops herself. "I kept meaning to—"

Alice keeps meaning to do everything in this apartment. It figures that when I try to help out, she feels she owes me an apology.

"It makes me feel useful," I say. "Like I'm doing something useful with my life."

"Do you want help? Giving meaning to your life?"

I don't. The search for meaning is complicated enough without additional parties getting involved, but the dishes go by quicker with her help, though my hands keep shaking.

"Noah," Alice says. She's noticed.

I hand her a fork I just washed.

"Noah," she repeats, louder. "When I came in here—you were smiling—you were thinking about him? Is that where you went?"

"I was thinking about doing the Macarena. It's all in the hips."

She lets out a sigh.

I am too much.

"It hurts," she says. I glance up in worry; new PPV symptoms usually mean the virus is adapting to the medication. "You push me away a lot," she explains. She dries the fork I gave her, replaces it in the silverware drawer. I listen to her thud up the stairs while in the background the rain patters lightly, the wind buffets our apple tree. Of course, the moment Alice leaves me, I miss her, I feel emptier. Her leaving is an ache in my chest, a shortness of breath. I want to yell after her, to tell her I'm terrible, to tell her I love her, but platonically. The sight of my blurry reflection in the kitchen window makes me queasy. Outside the rain falls harder, the apple tree bends. Without thinking I reach up, rub at my eye, get soap in it, and it burns.

"Fuck," I hear myself say.

What does it even mean, to *love* platonically? Is that just a nice way of saying *I'll never love you?*

I wash my eye out in the newly spotless sink.

"Thanks for the help," I whisper to Alice, though she is upstairs now and can't hear. I dry my face with the dish towel, after which I go up to my room, because my room has a door, and on this door there is a lock, and I use this lock to quarantine myself, so I can feel miserable in the perfect solitude of the gray walls that I call mine, without the risk of contaminating anyone.

Polo Club's key is on my nightstand, exactly where I left it.

I pull a pillow over my face so I don't have to look at it.

DREAMS OF DARWIN

Noah stumbles around and around Westing Lake, sipping at a bottle of vodka. His skin is peeling. He is falling apart, falling to pieces, which are scattered by the wind. On a hill overlooking the lake, a windmill spins.

A flock of finches appears on the horizon.

It grows larger.

Noah stares after the birds, brings the vodka to his lips. High above him, the windmill spins faster. It is a very picturesque windmill, and as the flock passes by, the windmill's blades picturesquely cut the flock to pieces. A hail of severed beaks, wings, feathers meanders to the ground.

A talon clips Noah in the arm, draws blood.

"Ow," he says.

Noah reaches to pick it up from the ground, holds it tight in his hand.

Overhead, a few finches have made it past the windmill. The males perform a mating dance to celebrate. The females accept or reject the males. Most of the males are rejected, and sulk. A small number of lucky couples proceed to mate and nest. The mothers lay eggs, guard them.

An occasional eagle drops out of the sky to make lunch of the happy parents.

Wind picks up, ruffling Noah's hair. Trees sway. A nearby branch cracks, tips, spilling a nest of eggs. The mother squawks, either in dismay or out of habit.

The remaining eggs hatch, grow into finches, who take off in a much smaller, more agile flock that does not fall prey to the windmill's blades, but that will eventually die out due to climate change. Noah knows he should feel triumphant at their momentary victory, but he does not. He bends down to bury that talon he picked up, only to find it has dissolved into dust.

"I will remember you," he says to the bird, but when he turns toward the lake, he is surprised to find he has no reflection.

He did not notice his own disappearance until he was already gone.

BEGIN WITH A LIE AND PROCEED

A few days pass before I have the nerve to bring up Zach to Alice. To tell her what I should've told her a long time ago. "Noah—" she lets my name hang there, at 11:52 p.m., in our kitchen, between the two of us, for a moment as real, as tangible as the scrambled eggs I'm having, the vodka-orange juice mixture I'm sipping. In eating an egg, I am not just eating one future chick. I am eating all the generations of chicks that would have followed from that chick. I offer her a bite, and she takes it. Swallows. We are eating generations together.

"We can talk about this tomorrow," she says. "You're eating. I'm glad you're eating, at least." Her eyes linger on the orange juice suspiciously.

I surprise myself by saying, "Let's talk about it now."

Generation after generation, new traits would accumulate and old traits would be weeded out until finally, new species would emerge, splinter off from the old. Alice looks away, stares at our floor, the crumbs on the floor, the crumbs that only Alice sweeps, because who has the time for sweeping, for brooms and feather dusters? Who has the time to *care*, when we are ending whole worlds with our gastric enzymes?

I say, "I'll do the floors tomorrow."

"Noah . . . I can't do this now. I don't—" She blows a strand of hair out of her face. "I already know. You had a friend. From the play. Juan. Okay?"

My mouth hangs open.

"He said—he told me—back in, back in April, just before the premiere. He came to see me and told me you loved someone else. He asked me to let you go. Okay?" Alice turns away.

"He told you—" I say.

"I knew this wasn't a good time—" she says, wiping at her eyes. "Knew this wasn't—I see the way you look whenever anyone mentions him. Don't you think I can see? And that time—there was this time you were walking back with him from the Wellness Center. You seemed so happy, I thought you might *skip*." She laughs, but there is no humor in it.

"Alice—"

"*You*. Skipping. Mr. Nihilistic Void of Nothing. Can you imagine that?"

"Nihilists are allowed to have a spring in their steps, too," I say. The joke is lame, I know, but I'm afraid of the very conversation I've started.

"I don't want you to be sad, Noah. That's the only reason I don't want you to drink. That's why I wanted you to talk to someone. You shouldn't have to drink to be happy, should you?"

"He's *dying*, Alice," I say, feeling a pressure building up inside me, the pressure of having to put on this silly act for so long. For no reason I can discern, I let my fork slip through my fingers and fall. We watch it for a few long seconds, lying on our dirty floor, until Alice bends to pick it up.

"Give it to me—" I say.

"Noah, I can—"

"Give it to me—"

"Be *careful*—"

After washing it off, I return to my seat. I continue to eat. I'm eating generation after generation, species after species, the first thing I've eaten since a bowl of soggy Cheerios and milk with a splash of vodka in the morning. Alice doesn't want me to die. It is a lot of work, not to die. The constant eating, for example. The cleaning, the dishwashing. The feelings. Having feelings is terrible. I am tired of them. Alice picks at a scratch in the table.

"You should tell him," she says. "How you feel."

I laugh.

"I'm serious, Noah."

"I don't think he feels the same."

"You can't know—"

"I do, though," I say, even though I don't believe my own words. I am simply speaking out my fear. If I speak my fears, they won't turn out true. "I should've always known. I'd send him these messages, on AwayWeGo, and he wouldn't always get back, or he'd get back to me in a few days, a week, and I was always the one who had the last word, and sometimes he'd forget and mention it when he saw me, say oh, I'm sorry, I'm really bad at keeping up, this and that, but the truth is, Alice, the truth is that if you love someone you respond to their message and you don't forget because it's so goddamn important to you, and you don't avoid them, because it's so goddamn important to you—"

"I need to go," Alice says, and before I can do anything, she's standing, and she's going to bed in her room, and she's not calling out to me, not asking me to come to bed with her, not brushing my hair out of my face or stopping me from picking at my cracked lips or giving me a good-night kiss.

That's how I know we've reached an end.

Tonight and for many nights after, I'll have my pillows all to myself. But when I set my half-finished vodka-juice concoction on my desk and fall into my bed, I'm afraid to close my eyes without the knowledge that someone needs me to open them again.

I turn on the lights and rip a piece of a page out of one of my notebooks.

Tell him, Alice said.

I give my pen a squeeze. It feels more meaningful this way, to shape the words, the letters, myself. But the paper stares at me accusingly, as does the key on my nightstand.

My room is full of accusation, and I can't think.

Tell him.

As if it were so easy, to arrange my words in the right order, the way Marty did for me in his play.

I down my vodka-orange juice concoction for inspiration.

Eventually, my pen moves.

I begin with a lie, and proceed from there.

> Zach,
>
> I'm writing this to you because I can't sleep.
>
> I guess I don't know what I want to say. Maybe I should write a list. Like, a brainstorming thing. I guess the truth is I need you to tell me you want to see me. I need to hear that from you. Or I need you to tell me you don't want to see me.
>
> It just feels like. You're very ~~erratic~~ confusing. I don't know what to do or what you want from me.
>
> Are you scared? Did you feel something for me the night we raced that you weren't ready to feel? But don't you understand I'm the last person in the world who wants to hurt you?
>
> I'm scared, too.
>
> But we could be scared together, if you wanted.

Wouldn't being scared together be better than being scared alone?

I'm sorry if this is awkward. I'm sorry if I'm wrong. I had a nice time seeing you the other day. Thank you for everything: helping me find security, lending me your shirt, for sharing your clothes, for being my friend. Please let me know.

Noah

The next day, the weather column of the *Westinger* forecasts heavy rain for the evening; there is no mention of the F.L.Y. demonstrations, no call for protest. That's the problem with science, I think. It can only ever tell you stories about practical matters. It will tell you you'll need an umbrella for tomorrow, but won't tell you whether or not you should hold it over the boy you love to keep him from getting wet.

The protesters have packed the residential quad, holding placards under a sky that is, for now, entirely cloudless.

About fifty students in all.

I pass them on the way to Zach's, and for a moment I think I see Marty among them. The crowd shifts, and I lose him. Security officers stand at the sidelines of the demonstration, sweaty and miserable in their uniforms. A girl holds a poster that reads "Think you're free? Think again," while a boy waves "TERTIARY CARE = VIVISECTION." A pair of administrators stage a halfhearted counter-demonstration on a nearby strip of lawn, complete with the usual handouts: glossy tertiary care informational flyers featuring young, smiling hospice nurses posing in beautiful rooms; AwayWeKnow articles detailing how the Houston quarantine and the cyber-bullying death of Katrina Mackey transformed the National Recovery Program.

All I can think about is the note in my hand. I slip it under Zach's door in Clover, and as I do so, I feel unreal.

I am less than a fiction, because when I played Peter Pan in Marty's play, that was the only time I ever felt necessary. An audience waited on my every word. The story couldn't go on without me. If I stood still, so did the whole world.

It was nice.

Act 3: Scene 3

[*Peter and Wendy sit on the floor of Peter's room. It is dark and eerie. A blanket rests on a nearby chair. Outside the room, in the corridor, two sleepy soldiers guard the exit. From out of view comes the sound of approaching steps.*]

PETER

I can't see, Wendy. It's all gone
black now. I think they're going
to come for me now.

WENDY

Don't say that.

PETER

I want to go to Neverland forever.

WENDY

Don't say that. Tell me more about
how you don't understand EA Sports
Phil Mickelson's PGA Tour.

PETER

I don't understand—

[*The steps are louder, now. Wendy glances at her watch, grabs the blanket from the chair.*]

PETER

[*pulls the blanket over himself
and Wendy. Then rips open a
package of Skittles.*]:
—why anyone would choose golfing
as their vicarious professional
athlete fantasy? You might as well
be a bowler.

WENDY

I have an idea.

[*Wendy takes Peter's hand. The two stand, wrapped
in the blanket, clutching at Skittles in their free
hands. Skittles are slipping out of their grasp,
falling.*]

PETER

I can go alone.

[*The steps are deafening.*]

WENDY

Don't be stupid, Peter.

[*She pulls him into the corridor, toward the guards.
The guards shake themselves awake, yell out for the
children to stop. Instead, Wendy and Peter break into
a run. For a few moments, the only sounds are the
voices of the guards and the rumble of approaching
steps. Peter and Wendy move mutely through this noise,*]

toward the exit. The guards lower their weapons, aim.
And then, all sound stops. Wendy and Peter are mere
feet away from the exit and the soldiers guarding it.]

PETER
To die will be an awfully big
adventure.

[*The whole stage goes dark. There is no more Peter, no*
more Wendy, no more soldiers or hospital or illness,
no more outside or inside. There is only the light
patter of Skittles falling. A spotlight shines on the
Skittles, littered across the floor of the stage. The
red digits of a wall clock read 2:33 a.m.]

THE END

TEN MONTHS BEFORE THE CATACLYSMIC, FIERY, KIND OF CLICHÉD END OF ALL THINGS (OR NOT)

A BEAUTIFUL DAY FOR MINOR ACTS OF LARCENY

One day in late November, the campus cloaked in white, Zach pointed up at the construction workers doing some work on the wall near the main gate, and his eyes lit up.

"That's how we get out of here," he whispered.

Polo Club drew up around him. Our ranks had thinned out since the first few meetings. There were only six of us now.

"No fucking chance we get within a hundred feet of the main gate," Melanie said.

"Ladders," was Zach's response.

We barricaded ourselves inside the library, on the second floor, near a window that looked out over Main Gate. Toward evening, construction workers packed up for the night. They took the ladders down, and we spilled out onto the library steps just as they loaded the ladders into a truck and drove up in the direction of Galloway, then veered left.

"Only thing over there are the caf and the greenhouses," Grace said, hands on her hips. "I always wanted to work in the greenhouses, green thumb and everything and I know all about flowers, most people wouldn't know a stigma from an anther. I didn't get the job, but I'm not mad, just disappointed."

I nodded sympathetically, and whispered to Marty, "I once had a blue thumb. I think I slept on it wrong and cut off the circulation."

"I prefer my thumbs in their original color," Marty said.

A few days later, Polo Club met for an early dinner at the caf.

Sure enough, in time, the construction workers drove up to the cafeteria and then turned north, toward the greenhouse. We ran after them as fast as we could in our boots and winter jackets, arrived to watch from behind some trees as they unloaded their equipment, storing it in a shed halfway between the greenhouse and the north side of the wall. We were silent for a while after they drove off.

Finally Nigel tried the shed door, but it was locked. He frowned. "Yo, brosef," he said finally, clapping Zach on the shoulder. "I got me an idea. Follow me." He started trudging back up toward the Greenhouse, and we obliged him warily.

"Oh wonderful, our resident Edison has a fucking lightbulb," Melanie said.

"Nikola Tesla was the real genius," Marty whispered into my ear.

"Direct current," I scoffed, and shook my head in disapproval, to pretend I didn't care that Zach was only a few feet away. We were playing our avoidance game again, barely looking at each other during Polo meetings, passing each other by on campus in mutually acknowledged un-acknowledgment. My proximity to him was inducing feverlike symptoms.

Nigel snapped his fingers. "Attention, attention, listen up my peeps, and you might learn something. I worked at the greenhouse, student employment and all that."

Grace looked too flabbergasted to speak. "They hired *you*, over *me*?" she said softly, but Nigel didn't hear.

"Watering fields that need to be watered," he was saying, "plowing hoes that need to be plowed." He winked at Melanie as he said this. Melanie's response was to try kick to him. He dodged out of the way.

130

"So *violent*," Nigel said laughing.

"Him over me," Grace said to me, eyes wide with the anticipation of my sympathy.

"A universe of cosmic emptiness is not a meritocracy," I informed her sadly as Melanie kicked at Nigel again and made contact this time.

Grace beamed at Melanie. "I think this warrants a high five. *Girl power!*"

Melanie regarded Grace's hand like it was coated in biochemical waste. "No thanks," she said. "I don't subscribe to social conventions that involve touching other people."

"*Guys,*" Zach said in a nasal, placating tone. He said he had a cold, but nobody believed him. "What are we doing?"

Nigel had led us to the door of the greenhouse.

"So get this, okay, and hold on to your mofo-ing socks, because shit, groundskeeper-bro has a key to pretty much all the toys around here, including—" He nodded at the construction shed. "We just gotta steal that shit, am I right?"

"Let's think about this for a moment," Zach said, his voice cracking.

"No thinking necessary. Step aside, my brosefs from other mosefs." Nigel brushed past Marty and me. "I got this."

Before we could say a word, he'd already knocked.

Seconds later, the door opened, revealing an old man in a puffy blue jacket, with a tuft of nose hair peeking out of his right nostril. The old man squinted at Nigel in confusion. "And who might you be?" he asked, full of patience.

Nigel looked affronted. "Yo, could ask you the same question." To us, Nigel whispered, "He's not wearing his glasses."

"I misplaced them," the old man said, in a tone of utter despondence. He scratched at his nose hair.

"Gerry," Nigel said, putting a hand on the old man's shoulder. "It's me. Nigel. Your, like, favorite worker. Confidante. Mentee. Fellow Christ lover."

Gerry's eyes widened in recognition. "You drowned the basil," he said in reproach. "And the radishes. And the gardenias."

Grace snorted in disbelief. "Don't complain. You gave *him* the job. You got what you were asking for."

The old man blinked mournfully. "The radishes were to be a gift for the director."

"I would've done better with the gardenias," Grace said.

"Sir," Zach interceded, stepping forward. "I know it's awfully rude of us to drop by unannounced, but—God—it's really very cold out here."

The old man frowned at Zach's feverish complexion, chewed at the inside of his lip for a few long seconds. "Well. Well, all right then, son, why didn't you say so?"

He invited us into his closet-sized office, packed with books on gardening and forestry, in addition to a copy of Whitman's *Leaves of Grass*, which I naturally gravitated toward. There was only one chair, so we had to stand while he fiddled around with a coffeemaker on a cluttered tray-top table in the corner. Nigel pointed at the wall to our backs, where a dozen different keys hung.

One of those keys would open the shed. We could grab the construction workers' ladders and scale the walls. We could be free.

That was Zach's plan.

Nigel nodded at the keys, meaning he needed a distraction, so the rest of us huddled around the groundskeeper while he stood at the coffeemaker.

"This old thing," he mumbled under his breath, and tapped the coffeemaker on the side a few times. "Should've gotten a *Cuisinart*, but Lizzie buys me a *Mr. Coffee*. What are you to do?"

"Sir, would you like help locating your glasses?" Zach asked, and my stomach initiated circus acrobatics mode. I pretended to bury myself in *Leaves of Grass*, in a collection of poems called *Calamus*, until for once I was no longer pretending, until the stanzas and poems all ran together. . .

I proceed for all who are or have been young men . . . You are often more bitter than I can bear, you burn and sting me . . . Yet you are beautiful to me . . . you make me . . . think of death, Death is beautiful from you, (what indeed is finally beautiful except death and love?) I think it is not for life I am chanting here my chant of lovers, I think it must be for death . . . Sometimes with one I love I fill myself with rage for fear I effuse unreturn'd love, But now I think there is no unreturn'd love, the pay is certain one way or another, (I loved a certain person ardently and my love was not return'd, Yet out of that I have written these songs.)

"Sir," Zach repeated, and I was back in the groundskeeper's office. Marty threw me a look of concern but I shrugged him off, slipped the book back onto a nearby shelf. I was hot. I needed some air, but I couldn't leave, not yet. Nigel was still fiddling around with the keys.

Melanie cleared her throat violently. "Ahem hurry the ahem fuck up ahem."

"We can help you look—" Zach said, still going on about the glasses.

Why did he have to be so nasally considerate while *stealing*?

"'I can see all right," the old man said, pressing his finger gently against the one-square-inch time display. "Oh, I'm all right. I manage, that I do."

"I think the button you're looking for is the *on* button," Melanie said.

"A good button," Gerry agreed, and continued pressing the time display. He let out a sigh and was about to give up when Zach leaped to his side.

"Let me try," he said, and they hunched over the coffeemaker together. "I've always loved the first snow," he said. "Now if it only weren't so terribly cold. But I suppose you can't have everything in life."

Nobody said anything.

Melanie looked at Zach like he was crazy, and I couldn't stand it. *Effusing unreturned love.* Sweat trickled down my back. "Actually," I said, "there's such a thing as warm snow."

"Oh?" Zach said, brows raised and before he realized what he was doing he was looking at me, really looking at me, for the first time in what felt like weeks.

"It's called water," I said.

Zach laughed, and I didn't just melt, I phase-changed straight to plasma, like fresh snowfall on the surface of the sun.

From behind us came a noise, like Nigel had knocked into something. Gerry turned, and saw him standing at the opposite end of the office.

"Hey," he said. "What're you doing over there, son?"

Nigel pointed at a framed picture above the keys, the old man and a woman who might've been his daughter. They were fishing.

"Yo, what is that, G-meister, like, a ten-pounder?" Nigel asked, pointing at the fish in the daughter's hands.

"Oh, I don't know, maybe twelve," the old man said, his eyes misted over in thought. He turned back to the coffee machine. Soon we had cups of coffee in our hands, but no key. Nigel shrugged at us in resignation. But when we spilled out of the greenhouse into a snowy evening, he started skipping.

"Guess what I got," he said, and patted his coat pocket.

"No way in hell," Melanie said.

He drew out the key, wiggled it.

"Ladder time, boss man?" he asked, dropping it into Zach's outstretched hands.

Zach nodded, a faint smile on his lips.

The key slid easily into the lock. The door of the shed creaked open. I watched the greenhouse, waiting for the old man to stumble out, to yell at us, to call security, to get us kicked out of Westing and taken to alien laboratories for emergency spleen extractions. Zach stepped inside first, motioned us to follow. One last look back, and I shut the door behind us.

Boxes everywhere, cleaning supplies, tools, all piled over each other.

"Oh my gosh, I see them!" Grace said, already moving toward a corner that had three ladders leaned up against the wall.

My foot hit on something hard, and I looked down, squinted.

"Blazing Phoenix Fireworks" it said on the box.

"Leftovers from convocation day?" I said to Marty.

"Probably," he said with a nod. "You didn't even *see*. You were in bed the whole day. You hissed at me when I opened the blinds."

"I *heard* them," I said. "They made beautiful sounds."

"I brought you pizza from the cafeteria," he said.

"Did I tell you you're the best?"

He shook his head no.

"Martin dear, you're the best."

"I do try," he admitted.

"Marty, Noah, get over here!" Grace said.

We joined the rest of the group by the ladders. I reached out a hand to touch a cool metal step. Up these steps, and I could see my parents again, defy whatever plan the administration or the government or the great tragic powers of the world had for me. Zach met my eye. His sweat-slick face shone in the light from an overhead window.

He was going to say something to me, and I knew we'd be all right again.

He said, "We need to leave everything like it was. Don't touch anything."

THE SEARCH FOR INTELLIGENT LIFE

That night, Marty told me, "I know what'll cheer you up."

He logged on to AwayWeWatch and put on this sci fi flick, *Pulse, My Electric Heart*, about two robots who want to have children so badly that they adopt a toaster and name it Sandy. While the credits rolled, we lay in our double in Clover and rattled off all the things we wouldn't live to see: gene therapy, holograms, clones, terraforming Mars, virtual reality, centralized memory banks that store people's consciousnesses, switching between new and better bodies like cars.

"I don't think it's possible," I said. "I mean—statistically— what—the universe is ten billion years old?"

"Fifteen."

"Fifteen billion years old! Think about it, Marty-guy. If this stuff were possible, then at our current rate of technological progress, we'd probably get there in, like, five hundred or a thousand years."

Marty didn't respond, so I continued. "If the universe is infinite, and there are billions and billions of stars, there's got to be intelligent life. That's the argument, right?"

"Oh, if not here, then somewhere. You would hope."

"So I'm saying—think about it, Marty-guy. If there's intelligent life, then just statistically, pure statistics here, some of it must have, like, five hundred or a thousand or ten thousand years on us. Statistically."

"Statistically," he agreed.

"So, if that stuff is possible, they've already done it. If it's possible to become gods they've already done it; if they could teleport here right now and save us from Apep and turn us all into immortal gerbils, thereby ending our suffering, they'd have done it."

"Are hamsters different in any significant way from gerbils?"

"Completely different," I said with all the confidence of the rampantly drunk. "In all relevant senses."

"I had a hamster once when I was a kid. You know? He had a good soul. He really liked his wheel. I would ask about him whenever I wrote my family."

I made a conscious decision *not* to ask the question he wanted me to. "It would suck to be an immortal gerbil. What would be the *point*? If there's no greater meaning, right, no purpose, if it's only us, scrambling around on our wheels—"

"Did you ever think the aliens are waiting for the right moment to intervene and alter the course of our evolution, like in *Year Thirteen*?"

"Marty, I'm trying to make a point here about the meaning of all things and here you are, going off about the onset of puberty."

"I'll have you know *Year Thirteen* is an AwayWeRead Top Five Fall Debuts pick."

"Whatever it is," I said, pretending to be aghast. "it doesn't sound like a nineteenth-century Russian novel to me."

"I do read other things," he said. "Occasionally. For fun. I do read for *fun*."

"The Russians aren't fun?"

"I didn't say that," he said hastily.

We lay in the dark for a while, until he asked, "Do you know why I like the Russians?"

I ventured some guesses: "Vodka, existential angst, ennui, terrible marital situations . . ."

"My grandpa, he told me about growing up in the Soviet Union, memorizing everyone, Pushkin and Mayakovsky, for school. When I came here, I spent, like, my first whole week in the library, trying to read up on everyone he told me about. I think most kids write home. I believe that. They're just afraid to talk about it, at Westing. I don't really understand it. In my old recovery center it wasn't a big deal, writing your family."

"Reading their letters would make them real," I said. "I don't want them to be real." If they were real, then their loss would be real. "We're not real to them."

"Don't say that."

"We're *not*, though." I wanted to tell Marty that the separation between us and our parents, it wasn't about walls, it wasn't about conspiracies, it wasn't even about PPV. It was about our language, the stories built into our language. It was about fictional demarcations of difference, like sick and gay, when in fact we were all subject to the great tragic powers of the world. Language enacted its own quarantines, and the stories built into it weren't all roses and puppies—they could work great evils. They could push people apart.

"If I was writing a story I'd edit them out," I said.

"Good thing I'm the writer," he said, a laugh in his voice.

I rolled out of bed, crossed the room, and smacked him in the rump with my pillow. He smacked me back. We had a pillow fight, delirious from grand talk and lack of sleep, until we both collapsed on his bed, and I kissed him good night on the cheek.

THE METAPHYSICS OF GOODNESS

A few days later, I got a text, one of those invitations which are understood to be contingent upon delivery of an appropriate quantity of alcohol.

There were a lot of parties at Westing.

They were all the same party, in a way.

The same faces. The same rooms and apartments. The same AwayWeTunes.

The guy who sent me the invite, Raj Karesh, was vaguely cute.

I needed to stop thinking about Zach.

I needed to stop using Alice to make myself feel better.

So for a while, I skipped out on Polo Club.

I AwayWeWatched a lot of movies on my laptop. Homeless children being rounded up and harvested for their dreams. A world government that ends war, poverty, crime by implanting everyone with chips that monitor their behavior and location at all times.

I spent nights trying to catch Raj, who proved elusive.

On Christmas night I arrived at Galloway 407 armed with ample volumes of eggnog, and was welcomed like a hero, and drank like a hero while the DJ alternated between shitty songs from MaxBeats and shitty songs from the Farsiders—at one point I got up on a chair. It wobbled under my feet as I spoke:

"If I am to be harvested to save the life of some Columbia professor of art history living in SoHo or NoHo or MoFo, then the least I can do is pass along some cirrhosis as well."

AWAY WE TUNE
Lyrics Database: **The Farsiders—"The Other Side"**

The walls we live behind
The sick, the poor, the blind.
Everyone's so busy
Differentiating ugly from pretty.
Everyone's so glad
With the views from their heights,
They can't tell good from bad,
Or dark from the light.

So bring on the pills and the drink,
Weekend projects, fix the kitchen sink.
Bring on the duck confit in Le Chateaux,
All that's missing from life is a nice gâteau.

Children, children, you've got to choose!
Skip along your merry way,
Do the dishes, pretend to pray,
Pretend you're a color other than blue,
Or fuck the walls, come for a ride
We'll take you to the other side.

Flushed faces stared up at me with admiration. One of them spoke: "Get the fuck out of my holiday airspace, you bitch-ass."

I got my bitch-ass the fuck out of his holiday airspace.

Then I was making out with a profoundly annoying boy named Juan, because Raj had gone into a room with Cassidy, and this had left me with another small hole in my heart. It was deflating fast, my heart, so Juan would have to do. He was one of Marty's theater friends, the assistant director on Marty's spring production, but more interestingly, at nineteen and a half, he was a super-senior, a rare breed at Westing, since nobody stayed around that long. We hadn't started rehearsal yet, so I knew Juan only in theory, from a distance, but, longevity aside, my impression of him was that he was one of those effortlessly good-looking kids who know they're effortlessly good-looking, who do not appear affected by the meds at all; I disliked him on principle.

So one moment I had his tongue in my mouth in Galloway 407, and the next I had his tongue in my mouth in a room I didn't recognize, in a bed I didn't recognize. I put a hand on his chest, disoriented, unsure of how I'd gotten wherever I was, but he kept kissing me. He was in his boxers. I had only my jeans on.

"I'm a good person," he was saying, "Or shit, I try to be, yeah?" His hand was in my jeans, I realized, but I felt distanced from the situation, enough so that I started laughing, because my zipper was giving him trouble.

"I think it's—it's all relative," I said as he continued to struggle with my zipper, so I decided to help him, kicking my jeans off, onto the floor. But my words had given him a pause. He cupped my balls through the fabric of my underwear and asked, "Have you read Hume?" and I didn't know if I wanted my balls cupped or not. My balls and I were miles apart.

I nodded, though I wasn't sure what exactly I was responding to.

"Shit, I got so much hate on that guy," he said, laughing. "Fucking Hume. Okay, okay. Let's say for a minute or a second or whatever that you're right, Noah, yeah yeah? It's only society looking out for its own self-interest and individuals in society looking out for their own self-interest. Now tell me something. You ever love someone? 'O Romeo, Romeo, wherefore art thou Romeo,' AwayWeRead Romance Pick of the Minute, and you know. Just say yes. Say yes."

"I don't believe in love," I said. "I believe in porn."

"Of course you'd say that. How did I know he would say that? Look, whatever. Just pretend you're in love with me, yeah?" He shifted closer, put a leg over mine.

I could've left. But I knew I wouldn't. He was attractive enough that you could love him from a distance, as long as you didn't know him, like an actor or musician. But we were too intimate now for the possibility of love, though I liked the bristly feel of his leg against mine.

"You shave your legs," I said.

"There he goes again," he said, massaging my crotch. "Kierkegaard says irony is destructive. It's a defense mechanism. I get it, I get it, you're afraid to get hurt, so you respond to the world with lame-ass ha-has, yeah? Too much of that, though, and you lose the ability to be sincere."

I couldn't get over the feel of his leg stubble. "What brand do you use? I swear by Gillette, personally."

"Now imagine." He reached over and placed his hands on my throat. "If the person you love, like, in an AwayWeRead Romance Pick of the Minute, swooning every time he blinks his long-ass eyelashes in your general direction, imagine if he did *this* to you, right?" He gave me a push, and then he was on top of me. The bed bounced beneath us. I laughed, because I didn't know what else to do.

His eyes bored into me; he had his hands on my throat. "Are you prepared to say that the only reason your one true AwayYouLove shouldn't collapse your trachea is because society says don't do that shit or you'll get punished for it? Is that the *only* reason I have for not turning your pretty face a pretty little blue?"

I could feel his hard-on pressed against my stomach, and his leg stubble against my leg.

I was afraid.

More than that, I was afraid to tell him I was afraid. If I did, I'd lose control of the situation.

Three years ago, when I was still at Richmond, a Westing student named Mark Lanburger freaked out about the onset of tertiary stage symptoms—memory loss, seizures, dramatic impairment of vision and hearing. He walked into the Galloway common room one night and beat a kid to death with a pink vase.

So I said, "God, will you shut up and fuck me already?"

And he did.

The next morning, I wandered the campus.

The previous night had the tinge of unreality, but it hurt to sit. I waited in line at the Academy Café, massaging my neck, and brought my coffee to one of several benches by the fountain at the center of the Galloway gardens, snow crunching beneath my boots. I stood and sipped my coffee and studied my breath, the dedication on the bench: *In memory of our daughter, Kimberly Anne Holowitz, the light of our hearts.*

I would have to spend the day reading *Notes from the*

Underground for my class on existentialist literature tomorrow. I had cracked the book the other day, a slim volume, sampled the opening lines, approved of them.

"*I am a sick man . . . a mean man. There's nothing attractive about me. I think there's something wrong with my liver. But, actually, I don't understand a damn thing about my sickness . . .*"

The opening lines magnified themselves in my memory, followed me wherever I went, they were like a light in my heart, and still I procrastinated doing the actual reading, wandered more, ordered another cup of Academy coffee. The winter burned my face every time I went outside; I enjoyed the feeling; this, I realized, was what I had most anticipated about college: the rolling grounds. We had visited colleges with Jonathan, before he got sick.

The recollection surprised me. I doubted I could trust the vividness of the details.

He'd been sixteen, had finished high school early—a wunderkind. I had thought, on our visits to campuses along the East Coast, that colleges were like parks for young people. Mom and Dad had ordered sandwiches and coffee, Jonathan had guzzled an orange soda, given me a sip, I had spit it out in disgust and they had laughed.

Eventually, I collapsed into a chair at the Academy Café. I only noticed Zach after he rapped gently on the table to get my attention.

"Long time no see," he said, regarding me warily. "How's it going?" He hovered over an empty seat, as if waiting for my permission. He still had that pale, sickly pallor, but looked better, *brighter.*

"Hi," I said, bookmarking page ninety-seven of *Notes from the Underground* with my finger. I had a headache.

"Good Christmas?" he asked.

"Something like that," I said.

"Just got done with a dorm team meeting," he said, still hovering. "Let me tell you, Noah. The glory of public office? Not what they make it out to be."

I didn't understand what he was doing, but I didn't want him to leave, either. I was relieved to see him again, even if I didn't understand what he was saying.

"You mean," I said, racking my mind for a quip. "You mean you haven't slept with your secretary?"

"God, no!" he exclaimed, and took a seat. "That's just it! I don't get to do any of the fun stuff real political leaders do. I haven't even embezzled any funds yet. When I brought it up during a council meeting, they looked at me like I was crazy."

"They lack vision," I said. Maybe, if we acted like everything was normal, everything *would* be normal.

"That's the thing, though," he said, turning away to cough. "This whole student government via representative democracy—terrible system."

Everything *was* normal; acting made it so; the Believers were right all along; manifest your reality in the face of deadly comets, though it hurt to sit. Though too much irony, too much pretending, degraded your ability to be sincere.

Zach waved a hand in front my face. "You there, kid? I have important news."

"Another rodent mishap?" I said, before I could stop myself.

His face fell. "Look—" he started.

I looked.

In typical Zach fashion, he looked away.

"What, exactly, do you want from me?" I asked, and it felt good.

He exhaled a long breath, ran a hand through close-cropped hair. He spoke hesitantly, his voice growing quieter the longer he talked. "I just—wanted to tell you—new development."

"Okay," I said. "Tell."

"Well," he said, and risked a glance, a quick smile. "Melanie knows how to call our parents."

CALLING HoME ON NEW YEAR'S

Melanie had gotten her hands on the number for the Home Hotline.

The first part—*876691—allowed you to dial out of Westing.

From there, 1-72-CALL-HOME would connect you with an operator who would then connect you to your parents.

What if they knew where the sick kids went? Would I want to know? And what if they asked to see me?

We decided to call our parents together, on New Year's Eve.

I spent the evening pre-gaming and reading the comments section of an AwayWeKnow article titled "New Data on Hazardous Asteroid Headed for Earth." jimbo_the_jumboshrimp9 stated that the asteroid would hit, the dead would rise up from the ground, Jesus and the Antichrist would have their long-awaited pissing contest in the land of milk and honey and nuclear warheads. BoobsInaTube asked if jimbo_the_jumboshrimp9 was an alias for Morgan, president of the Believers. jimbo_the_ jumboshrimp9 declined to either confirm or deny that assertion.

Later, Polo Club barely fit in Zach's room. By midnight, empty bottles of beer and hard alcohol littered the floor—the drunker we were, the less scary it would be to make the call. Melanie had even sported a celebratory pink bow for the occasion.

"I feel like this is *it*," Nigel was saying. "Fucking *it*. The beginning. My life starts here, bros. Not there. It's here. First day of the rest of my capital L longevity-challenged life. Shit, you know what I mean?"

And then he and Grace were kissing.

Melanie made a gagging sound, mumbled, "I hope you have Plan B, because I wouldn't trust lover boy over there to put his socks on right."

Grace threw up the international one-finger-signal for mind-your-own-ovaries.

"Oh shit," Melanie said. "Miss 'Oh my gosh I have a green thumb sprouting like a tulip out of my ass' knows the one-finger salute."

Zach regarded the make-out session from his bed with a bemused, cross-eyed expression; he was in one of his quiet moods, had withdrawn into himself. He raised a weary, resigned eyebrow at me, but I didn't feel like playing decipher-the-subtext today. I could almost feel Juan's mouth pressed against mine; we hadn't hooked up since that one night, but I knew we could. He kept sending me messages on AwayWeGo, and that made me feel like I belonged in my body, that I wasn't just some ghost flickering in and out of matter. There was no good reason to see him again, and many good reasons against it. But I needed to be needed. Otherwise, why stay? Camus said that all philosophy was an attempt to answer that question, Hamlet's to be or not to be. Why bother with the slings and arrows of outrageous fortune? The scorn of time? The pangs of despised love?

I turned away from Zach, leaned into Marty-guy, who was at my side, the two of us at the foot of Zach's bed, and said, "If you think about it, *every* moment is the beginning of the rest of your life."

"Whoa, Noah. *Whoa,*" Marty said. "You should start an AwayWeBlog."

I laughed. Self-help blogs were the lastest AwayWeGo epidemic, kids you'd watched streak through the Westing campus doling out advice like *Make a List of 5 Things You're Thankful for Every Day* and *PPV Isn't The Only Thing That's Contagious. Remember to Smiiilleee.* ☺

"Marty and Noah's E-guide to Happiness and Personal Growth," I proposed.

He nodded in excitement, nearly losing his glasses in the process.

"Step one," I said. "Buy a bottle of vodka."

"I'm trying to be more sober," he slurred mournfully, while sipping at an empty bottle of beer.

"You're doing an admirable job," I said.

"Have I ever told you"— he squinted at me—"that you have a great nose?"

I put a hand on Marty's leg. "Step two of Noah and Marty's E-Guide to Happiness and Personal Growth is to compliment each other's noses and buy a copy of the *Kama Sutra*."

"Step three—" Melanie said, as Grace and Nigel continued sucking on each other's faces, "the day-after pill." Melanie covered her eyes with her arm, her shoulders heaving with what I thought was laughter.

Grace responded with another mind-your-own-ovaries gesture.

"Step four: Turn to page sixty-nine." I gave Marty a wink.

He either winked back or had lost control of his facial muscles. "One of the finest noses I've ever *seen*."

"Hey, Noah—" Zach said.

I ignored him.

"I think I want to call home," Melanie said, quiet, wiping at her face with her sleeve. Her bow bobbed.

Outside our door, sounds of partying. Laughter. Shouts. Feet thudding in the hallways. Security didn't care. Their job was to keep us inside the walls. Marty broke our silence by saying, "Some animals don't die. I was reading. Crocodiles. Also jellyfish. They are beyond death."

Nobody responded to Marty-guy, so I had to. I observed, rather astutely, "We have to keep dying. Otherwise, what would the funeral-industrial complex do? Can you imagine the loss of jobs?"

"Crematoria workers, begging on the streets, coffin makers unable to feed their children," Zach pitched in, and I couldn't help it. I laughed.

"Why, the ancient and honorable trade of urn making would cease to be a commercially viable enterprise," I said. *"Besides.* We need to make room for babies."

"I want to call home," Melanie said.

"Noah," Zach said, "I've heard it takes a good seven minutes for your brain to shut off after the rest of your body dies. Maybe that's where it all comes from. All the—myths and legends and religions and . . ." He trailed off.

I hated Zach for looking at me the way he was looking at me, for saying something so perfect. The stories we told, and the words they were composed of, they all fell short of capturing the world, the same way that "sick" could not capture any one of us here, the way that "sick" was a story the outside told about us, the way that "boy I love" was a story I told about Zach, the way "just a friend" was a story he told about me. But Camus said to live meaningfully was to acknowledge our condition—the fact that we had all these contradictory stories and no way of knowing which was right.

"What do you believe in?" I asked him.

"I believe in *you,*" Marty-guy said into my ear, ruining the moment.

151

"You guys are killing me," Melanie said. "I WANT TO CALL HOME." She seemed surprised when we all turned our glassy-eyed gazes on her. She wiped at her face with a sleeve again.

"Hey, maybe tonight's not actually the best—" Zach started in his placating-leader tone. He gestured at the state of us. Nigel broke off making out with Grace to let out a triumphant belch.

But Melanie already had her phone in her hands, set to speakerphone. The only sound in the room was the dial tone, the clicking of the keys—she entered the dial-out number—dial tone again. She entered the operator's number.

I held my breath. On the third ring, I noticed the tear lines on her cheeks, illuminated by the glow of her screen. I opened my mouth to say something, but before I could, a familiar voice filled the room:

"Welcome to Away We Call Wireless. We are sorry, but your number cannot be completed as dialed. Please check the number and dial again."

Silence.

"Melly-baby, you *dialed* it wrong," Nigel said, but Grace shushed him.

Melanie dialed the number again.

"Welcome to Away We Call Wireless. We are sorry, but your number cannot be completed as dialed. Please check the number and dial again."

"I thought you said you called—" Nigel said, but Grace elbowed him.

Melanie was shaking.

"Welcome to Away We Call Wireless—"

"Welcome to—"

"Welcome—"

"Wel—"

Zach got up from his bed, pried the phone gently from her hands, and wrapped his arms around her. She leaned into his chest, crying, and my heart thumped *I love him* and *I love him* and *I love him.*

"I thought you fucking said—" Nigel started again.

"You all think I'm a bitch," she said, gasping, "and I just wanted—I knew you were all chickenshit and I just wanted you to believe—I wanted to believe—"

She didn't finish the thought.

Zach left to walk her to her room, and in the interval Marty fell asleep on my shoulder, drooled on me a little. I kept checking his pulse to make sure he was alive. Zach returned, stood in the doorway with a downcast expression. Our cue to leave. I shook Marty awake lightly, though it felt like I was the one who was asleep. I was still reeling, struggling to understand. Did we have the number wrong? Or was there no number at all? Nigel kept saying, "I don't get it, babe." Grace had to practically carry him out of Zach's room and down the corridor, his arm draped around her neck, because he couldn't stand on his own.

I peeked out of Zach's room to stare after them. "You two be safe now," I called, trying to lighten the mood.

"Not nice, Noah," was Grace's reply.

"Baby, it was a joke, and pretty *l-m-a-o* if you ask me," Nigel slurred. He gave me a thumbs-up, and they disappeared, around the corner.

A couple seconds later I felt a tap on my shoulder. Marty's wide eyes took me in, and he said, with the slow deliberation of a drunk trying not to sound drunk, "I will give you and Zachary a private moment." He stumbled off down the hallway, pitching first to one side, then another.

So it was just me and Zach. I wanted to close his door, but I didn't. It gaped open, spilling light at my feet.

"Happy New Year, kid," Zach said with a sad smile.

"That was kind of you," I said.

He winced, shook his head. "God, I'm a terrible person. I'm terrible to you. I'm just—I'm just very confused."

"You wanted to connect us to our parents."

"I don't know why you like me."

I tried to find the words to explain, to tell him it mattered that we were sick, that we were standing here, comets and PPV and all, that we'd wanted to call our parents together, whether or not we could've pulled it off, whether or not there was ever a magic number you could dial to connect you to them. It mattered that we'd done all that together.

"Was she okay?" is what I asked instead.

"She's pregnant," he said, playing with his collar. "They're making her—they're making her end it."

I nodded stupidly.

"The baby would be infected," he said. "They don't live past the first few months when they're born with it."

I didn't know whether he was explaining why they were making her end it, or why it was *okay* that they were making her, so I nodded some more, waiting, but Zach had run out of things to say.

"Did you think it would work?" I asked. "The Home Hotline, I mean?"

"Oh, I don't know," he said with a sigh. "Who knows? I don't know what I'm doing most of the time. I figured you'd know that by now."

I was afraid to go for a kiss, so I hugged him.

"Noah, I—"

154

"Can we just stay like this awhile?" I asked.

He let out a sigh. "We can stay like this," he said.

And we did.

We stayed until he said, "Tell me why you like me. Why me of all possible people. I'm not even that great. I mean, I've met better specimens of humanity. I can list half a dozen off the top of my head."

"How much time do you have?"

I felt his laugh pass out of his body and into mine.

"So cheesy," he said.

"As cheesy as that dystopian I saw you AwayWeReading in the caf the other day?"

"Hey." He pulled back to regard me with mock sternness. "*Final Flight* is a tour-de-force that's impossible to put down. It says so in the blurb."

"Uh-huh."

I felt closer to him than ever, but he pulled away from me, brought his hands to his head, massaged his temples. He turned his back to me to look out at the crescent moon hanging in his window. "God, I was supposed to be better than this. My mom was this executive at IBM. She was always saying how I had so much privilege, I ate privilege and I shit privilege and if you don't do something with it you're a waste. I'm sitting here doing nothing. We still don't know where we go when we go away."

"Why does what your mom thinks matter?"

"You don't understand, kid." He shook his head. "People like her make the world go round. They're the ones who get to be remembered."

I came up behind him, wrapped my arms around his waist, but he brushed me off. I stumbled into his desk.

"I'm sorry," he said. Then, "I feel like, like I'm spinning and

I'm spinning and I don't know where I'm going. Round a rosy, pocket full of posies, ashes, ashes, we all fall down."

He spun and spun and let himself fall down.

I hesitated, but only for a moment.

I followed suit, landing beside him.

"We're crazy," he said, laughing.

"Yes," I agreed.

In my pocket, my phone went off.

A text from Alice.

Happyyy New Year. :) :) :) I am so happy to have a friend like you in my life, Noah.

Marty and Noah's E-Guide to Happiness and Personal Growth

5 Super Tips for a Healthier, Happier YOU

1   Your life is a reflection of YOU. Take a good look inside yourself. If you don't like what you see, there's always the age-old remedy of hallucinogenic substances.

2   Avoid the study of history. Why should the ancient Aztec practice of human sacrifice (by evicting the heart from its typical place of residence inside the chest cavity) put a downer on your mood today?

3   At least once a day, think of a happy memory. If no such memory comes to mind, make one up. Failing that, turn to immortal uplifting words of Nietzsche: "The thought of suicide is a great consolation; in this way one can get through many a bad night."

4   When a relationship doesn't work out, remember, it's not you, it's them. All sixteen of them. Seventeen including your mother, whose last words to you were, "I hate your face."

5   Most of all, make an effort to see the humor in all things. Stage III cancer is serious business, but your radiologist's handlebar mustache doesn't have to be.

THE POSSIBILTY OF OKAY

We played ring-around-the-rosie together, and now he was ignoring me.

The new year unfolded into days of fresh snow, long blue skies. I read Marty's play over and over again, went on a couple lunch dates with Alice. In mid-January, Polo Club walked Melanie to her appointment on the third floor of the Westing Wellness Center. I should've been thinking about Melanie, but I kept glancing at Zach.

"I hate days like this," Melanie said. She paused briefly at a window by reception before signing herself in. It was late afternoon, and the cars in the parking lot had begun their steady stream out the main gate.

"What's the world's *problem*?" Nigel asked, sipping a root beer that I was pretty sure was diluted with something extra, because he wobbled his way to the waiting room. "I mean, sometimes I wanna slap the shit out of it."

"Honey," Grace said, leaning into Nigel's ear. "I love you, but shut those pretty lips."

Melanie settled in a corner of the waiting room and proceeded to study her hands. Zach sat down next to her, whispering into her ear, prompting frequent eye-rolls as well as an occasional smile. Melanie looked up in surprise as Marty and I sat down on her free side.

"It's not right," Marty said, barely audible. "Them making you, I mean."

158

"It's not like I'd even want it," Melanie said, and cleared her throat. "I don't want it. I'm glad, actually."

Marty opened his mouth but nothing came out, so I jumped in.

"You don't have to want it to want a choice," I said.

Zach scratched his nose very solemnly.

"I don't know why you're all talking in whispers," she said, and stared at me, daring me to deny it. "You, too," she said, turning on Zach. "I'm not *fragile*. I don't need you to handle me with kiddy gloves. I don't even need you here. I'm happy to be here."

"We're here because we like you," I said, trying to lighten the situation, but she rolled her eyes and said, "*Ugh*. That's something *he* would say," she said, nodding at Zach.

A nurse with a clipboard peeked into the waiting room. "Melanie Wong?"

Melanie stood, hesitated at the threshold. "You don't have to wait for me."

"We will, though," Zach said. When she'd gone, he turned to Marty and me. "That was nice of you. I was—in a state of oscillation. As an elected officer, there is always the dilemma about how to best represent your constituents." Zach hesitated briefly. "Noah, at the last Polo meeting. Your square knots were magnificent, I must say. I don't think I ever properly commended you. I wanted to commend you."

I smiled stupidly, because everything was going to be okay, but Marty spoiled it by breaking off from his blank gaze long enough to confide in me that he had "rarely seen better."

"Seriously, bro," Nigel said, from across the waiting room. "You put us to shame, man. To *shame*—" He had spilled some root beer on his shorts.

"You guys are haters," I said, but it felt wrong, to joke, to love, while Melanie was in another room, preparing to have the contents of her uterus gently suctioned out, emptied out—this was how a brochure on a nearby table described the procedure.

Aspiration.

"I've failed you guys," Zach said, scratching sheepishly at his head. "But I think I know how to make everything right." He motioned to Grace and Nigel, who gathered round.

"Our phones," he said, keeping his voice low. There were a couple other girls in the waiting room. "If we snuck them out, when they come to take us away—it's not like they're going to strip-search us when we're lying there dying, right?"

"Bro, what you even talking about?" Nigel said, and burped.

"Our phones," Zach repeated, slow. "We know we can only call Westing numbers. We don't know we can't call Westing numbers from *outside* Westing. It wouldn't even need to be a call. Just one text. We could text each other what's it like. Where the sick kids go when they go away. The tertiary centers." He had a hint of a smile on his face. "God, it's so simple."

"A friend of mine said—" Grace hesitated, adjusting her Westing Rugby sweater. "She said she thinks they take us straight to a crematorium." Grace seemed as surprised as us, like she hadn't meant to voice the thought.

I thought of Alex, how he said it would be better if the world were simply rid of us, so we wouldn't be a burden on anyone anymore, not on our parents, nor the taxpayers.

"I wouldn't be surprised," Marty said somberly. "I mean, look what they're doing to Melanie. I mean, I *get* the baby wouldn't, the baby probably wouldn't, I know that—"

"I can still make everything right," Zach said, finally, and our eyes met. My stomach did one of its usual Zach-flips.

"Man, I read the other day on AwayWeKnow, some dude with a prosthetic leg punched a shark in the face," Nigel said. "World makes *no* fucking sense, am I right?" He had finished off his root beer concoction, was now playing with the empty bottle, trying to screw on the cap, failing. "Punching a shark in the face. What have *you* done in your life?"

Grace shrugged, and emphasized what we should take away from Nigel's spiel: "He was reading."

"So we have to wait until one of us gets sick," I said. "Before we know where the sick kids go."

Zach nodded. "Only way I can think of."

Outside on the Galloway lawn, a handful of students were having a snowball fight. The sun receded and my stomach grumbled, the sky turning a bruised color, the last of the teachers' cars gone, and after a little while of this, I offered to go grab some dinner for us all. Zach said he'd join me, so we set off in the cold together; it was the first time we'd been alone since New Year's.

Our boots pressed softly into the snow. The cafeteria loomed large before us. We stole glances at each other while pretending we weren't stealing glances at each other. At the cafeteria steps, he pressed a hand into my shoulder.

"Noah." He bit his lip. "I'm going to tell you something that's going to make you hate me, but I think you need to hear it, okay?"

"Okay," I said, and there was a man inside my chest, doing a drum solo on my heart.

"Last night, I was sitting there and I imagined I was talking to you, kid. The whole back and forth. I say ra ra ra and you bring your hand to your ear, pretend you don't hear and then I say it again. The whole shebang. And I could see everything. I could see your expression, I could hear the way you'd say things, I knew what you'd say, and I'm sitting there thinking about all this and I realize I love you."

I blinked stupidly at him, my mind drawing a total blank.

"But I think," he said, as students shouldered past us, "it's platonic."

I slumped down onto the steps, holding the railing for support.

"When I met you, I was confused, and I think you were confused, too, because you're one of my favorite people, kid, you really are. One of my favorite people *ever*."

I didn't answer.

There were too many words, and I was trying to order them, make sense out of them.

He loved me.

"I'm sorry, that was a bit of a twist ending there. I'm sorry, Noah."

Snow from the steps seeped into my jeans. "I don't understand." We had played ring-around-the-rosie together and raced through the rain. We had our ra ra ras. He loved me, but he didn't want to be with me, because my skin was peeling. Because I was not beautiful.

"Noah, it's not fair to you, I know, I know. It took me a while to figure out. I'm just—not that way, I don't think. If you don't want to see me again . . ."

"You push me away a lot. Are you pushing me away?"

He shook his head. "I don't think that's it, kid. It's not fair to you, I know. If you don't want to see me again . . ."

"Stop saying that, *please*."

I wanted to tell him it didn't matter. If he loved me, why should anything else matter? But it wasn't just one man playing my heart like the drums. It was an entire percussion-only orchestra, and they were playing faster and faster, rising toward a crescendo. I wanted to tell him we could love each other without me ever touching him, that we couldn't touch each other anyway, metaphysically, electrons repelling and all that, he could sleep with anyone he wanted to, as many girls as he wanted to, Addie or no Addie, I didn't care, things could be okay, even if Zach didn't love me, sitting there with the snow soaking into my jeans I needed to believe in the possibility of okay, I needed to believe in a story that ended with "And then they lived happily ever after," but Zach was bending over me, he was saying something I couldn't hear or didn't want to, I had heard enough, so I heaved myself up and began to run in the direction of the frozen lake. I made it a dozen steps before I slipped, nearly fell, caught myself with one hand against the ground, began to run again, because I needed to be someplace other than where I was, someone other than who I was, I needed to feel the ache in my body to remind myself that I was real.

That night, my phone went off at two in the morning.

A group message from Melanie.

emergency. meet at greenhouse.

I groped in the dark for my clothes, pulled them on.

"Marty," I hissed. *"Marty."*

He grumbled in his bed, stirred.

His phone lay on his nightstand, buzzing. He fumbled for it, missed. It clattered to the floor.

"Ugh," he said.

I shook his shoulder gently.

"Come on," I said.

"Whuzgoinon," he mumbled, reaching for his glasses.

"Something's wrong with Melanie." I shoved my phone in his face, and he squinted at the bright of the screen. But it got him moving, good old Martin. He stumbled out of bed and toward the dresser, wrestled with his clothes.

"Nightvision'snogood," he mumbled as he turned a shirt this way and that.

I hit the lights.

We both winced, but he said "Thanks," and threw me a lopsided smile while I called Melanie.

No answer.

I found Zach in my contacts, my thumb wavering over the Call button.

I flipped my phone shut.

The corridor outside our room was dimly lit. I headed for a fire exit, taking the stairs two at once, Marty right behind, pushed through the heavy metal door at the rear of Clover and into falling snow.

"Is she okay?" he asked.

"She's not answering," I said.

We began to run toward the greenhouse, but Marty couldn't keep up. I hesitated, listening to his heavy breathing, his footsteps on the path behind me, the air between us filled with floating orange specks lit by nearby lampposts.

"Go on," he gasped.

So I did.

I ran as fast as I could. I ran behind Galloway, along the forest path, the trees high and dark and casting shadows in the night, my feet pounding, the snow heavy now, the air so full of it, the wind nearly strong enough to blow me off my feet, so caught up in the moment, in the joy of being alone and young and fast, the joy of stars in the winter, I actually *laughed*. The walls in the distance, lit by lamps and moonlight, bobbed with every step I took, until I slowed up to the greenhouse, the shed by the greenhouse, the figures by the shed. I could barely make them out—they were shadows—but I made out their voices.

Zach and Melanie, arguing.

"You're not thinking clearly," he was saying, his tone desperate.

She pushed him in the shoulder. "Did you bring it or not?"

I drew up a few feet away.

Zach glanced pleadingly at me. "She wants to make a run for it."

"That's what we're here for, right? Polo Club," she said. "Or was that a bunch of bullshit? Just a stupid little game. Did you even bring it?

"I brought it," Zach said, quiet.

"Or was this all just an excuse for you two lover boys to gaze dreamily into each other's eyes?"

"Maybe we should think about this," I said.

"I'm done thinking," Melanie said. "I'm done with these walls and these people." She softened briefly. "If I think about it, I'll never do it."

Zach reached out to touch her, but she brushed him off, lunged for his pocket. They struggled and I watched them struggle. All that talk about saving people, about having a fail-safe. Why not? Why not do it now? Except we were sick. More children might end up behind walls, because of us.

"It was a game," I said. "It was never real, Melanie. It was just fun. Just a little harmless fun."

They turned to me with surprise.

"Noah," Zach said slowly. "You're—you're mad."

"I am," I admitted. I was sleepy and hurt and felt like

someone had made me up on a whim, without much care or forethought.

"Great," Melanie said, and let out a harsh laugh. "Great time for a lovers' spat, guys."

"We're not—" Zach said. "Melanie, *please*. I thought we were friends."

"Do you have the key or not?" she said.

Steps crunched from behind. I turned. Several figures were scurrying toward us.

"So what's the emergency, my peeps?" Nigel called out, but for once, his levity sounded forced. The figures materialized into Nigel, Marty, and Grace. Marty was breathing hard; he looked like he might collapse from the exertion.

"I'm getting out of here," Melanie declared. "Zach was about to unlock the shed for me, weren't you, Zach?"

"If you run now," Zach said slowly, "the rest of us, we might not get another chance."

"Come with me," she said to all of us, pressing a glove to her face. "Or was this just a game for you guys? A fun little diversion. Like Board Game Club. Was this Board Game Club?"

"Melly-baby, you're not thinking about one fundamental piece of data, right?" Nigel said. "It's *cold* out there." He pointed at the walls, only a hundred feet from where we stood.

"Honey," Grace said into his ear. "God bless you, I love you, but shut those pretty lips." To Melanie, "Zach came up with a great plan, didn't you, Zach? Tell her about your plan."

Zach explained about waiting for someone to get sick. "All it'll take is one text, and we'll know where the sick kids go."

"Or we could go now," Melanie said. "Have you *seen* those tertiary care flyers they pass out? *Incontinence support*. I don't fucking want to wait around for *incontinence support*. A glorified hospice. That's where the sick kids go. To have their diapers changed 'cause they shit themselves every three hours. That's where we go, guys. Open your fucking eyes. Smell the goddamn roses. An immigrant lady with broken dreams of a better future. Will wipe your chafing ass. So she can send her kids to college. That's it."

"If we don't let her go, we're no better than the administration," Marty said. "The government." He added, "I'll go with you."

"Marty?" I asked, feeling sick.

"There you go. Someone else actually has balls," Melanie said. "Zach, *give me the key*. Or admit to everyone here that your butt-buddy was right. This was never about giving us a choice. It was your stupid little power trip where Zachary gets to make all the rules and feel special."

"Don't say that," I whispered. "I didn't say that."

Zach had his head in his hands. I couldn't tell if he was crying. I watched him, all of us did, all of us rooted in the knee-deep snow by the construction shed in a silent circle, the stars bright pinpricks overhead. He stuffed a hand into his pocket and drew out the key.

Melanie unlocked the door, shoved the key back in his face. She turned to us.

"Who's going to help me?"

I needed to get away from Zach, so I stepped forward. He shot me a hurt look, but I didn't care. Melanie and I stumbled into the pitch black of the shed, knocking into boxes and tools, wouldn't it be a ball if we knocked into the fireworks and set them off, burned the whole shed down? A fitting end to the night. Within a few minutes we had two ladders leaned up against the front of the shed.

Melanie nodded to the nearest section of the wall. She tried to heave a ladder by herself. I rushed to help. Marty joined us. The rest of Polo Club grabbed the second ladder, and side by side our two groups began the quiet trudge in the direction she'd indicated.

This was not how Polo Club was supposed to end.

I wanted say something.

To take back what I'd said to Zach.

I didn't know how.

"Marty," I whispered. "*Why?*"

"She can't go alone," he said simply. "Nobody deserves that."

Melanie, holding the front end of the ladder, stiffened, stopped.

The walls were in front of us now, illuminated by lampposts running down their entire length. Zach, Grace, and Nigel trudged to a stop beside us with their ladder, and we all stood looking up, and it struck me how *small* the walls were, only about ten or twelve feet, how easily I could slip over them.

What would be waiting for me on the other side?

We were close now. Little red lights flashed along the top of the wall, spaced out every few feet. I'd heard stories about motion sensors and cameras, also laser-guided missiles and automatic machine guns, but had never gotten near enough to investigate.

"We've got to hurry," I said.

"My man-muscles hurt," Nigel said. "Can we at least set the ladders *down*?"

"Do you still want to do this?" Zach called.

"I don't know," Melanie said. She lowered her end of the ladder to the ground; Marty and I followed her lead. She walked up to the wall, touched it, rested her head against it, like she was praying. Marty took a few steps toward her, but maintained a distance. "I don't know," she repeated. She reached out, touched Marty's shoulder, even though she didn't subscribe to social conventions that involved touching other people.

"You're sweet," she said. "I think I like you most of all, but I don't think you like me."

Before Marty could say anything, the blare of a siren pierced the night.

From somewhere on the wall, a mechanical voice: "Students. Your proximity has been detected. Please step away from the wall immediately and await incoming security personnel."

"We've got to go," I said. "Either stay or go."

Melanie gave Marty a brief kiss on the cheek, and said, loud, "I can't. You're right. Congratulations." She laughed bitterly. "I don't want to die."

She turned on her heel and began to run in the direction of the residential quad. Security had to stick to the trails, but we did not. We could make it. Polo Club began to scatter. But Zach cried out: "*Wait. We need to put the ladders back! They'll know if we don't.*"

It was too late. The others couldn't hear him, but I did. We exchanged glances. He picked up one end of a ladder and looked at me, begging without saying a word.

"They already know, Zach," I said. I waved at the red lights. "They probably got it on camera."

"Help me," he said simply, without letting go of his end of the ladder.

So I did, even though it was pointless. I picked up the other end and we ran, carrying it to the shed. A dozen feet from the door Zach tripped, dropped his end.

"Fuck," he said.

He dug it out of the snow and we went on, practically threw it inside the shed, against the nearest wall, but it pitched forward. I grabbed an edge; my grip was awkward. The ladder leaned further, about to fall. Zach's hand caught the other side just in time, and we set it against the wall again, better this time, our breaths coming in gasps.

"The second one," I said.

"God," Zach said, and took off for the wall again, me by his side.

Tonight I was faster.

The second ladder wasn't slumped in the snow anymore.

Marty hadn't scattered like the rest. He had righted the ladder by himself, set it against the wall, and now he stood, perched on the top step, looking out beyond Westing.

"Please step away from the wall immediately and await incoming security personnel," the mechanical voice intoned.

"Marty!" I yelled up at him.

He turned, peered down at me. I knew he was considering whether to stay or to go.

The siren was closer. The security carts revved in the distance, and Marty made his decision.

He descended the steps, jumped to the ground.

Zach had drawn up by now. The three of us ran for the shed, the ladder slippery in our gloved hands. I was in the lead. I kicked open the shed door, took a step, but the ladder hit on something. *Stuck.*

"Noah," Zach said desperately.

"Trying," I said. "Take a step back."

We managed to unpry the ladder. Something tumbled to the ground with a terrible clatter, and I had to step over it, but finally we had the ladder inside the shed, finally Marty shut the door.

We heard the security carts.

I shuffled toward a dark corner, bent over, crouched, Marty and Zach following. Hit my head on something hard and saw flecks of light. Someone bumped into me from behind and I nearly fell. We threw ourselves behind some cardboard boxes just as the door squealed open.

Steps scraped against the floor. A flashlight flared.

"They're here," a man said, and for a moment I thought he meant us, until his flashlight settled on the ladders. "Kind of them to pick up after themselves."

The steps came closer. A second flashlight beam illuminated a pair of rakes and garden shears five feet from where we sat hunched together.

One of the guards cleared his throat, spit.

"Stupid fucking kids," a second voice said.

"Ah, they don't know what they're doing," the first man said. "Prob'ly a prank. 'Member the dumb shit we got into as kids?"

"Stupid fucking kids," the second voice said. "Didn't even get a good shot of them, all this dark and snow."

"Nope," the first man affirmed. Then, "Hey, Jim, you're a poet."

"Shut the fuck up, Langdon," Jim said. His voice even closer now, his flashlight drifting over my head. Zach and Marty trembled into me, and I trembled into them. I held someone's hand.

"Let's go back," Langdon said, and his steps receded. "I want to finish my coffee 'fore it gets too cold."

Jim let out a sigh, and turned to follow. The door squealed shut, but I held my breath until the security cart engine started up again, before fading into the winter quiet.

I stayed hunched in that corner for a long time.

I stayed hunched in that corner until a pair of hands encircled me. I jumped at the touch, but relaxed into Zach's embrace. He pulled me back, until I was sitting between his legs, his arms wrapped around me.

He set his chin on my shoulder.

He whispered warm breath into my ear: "Thank you for staying."

A few feet away, Marty sat huddled into himself.

I reached out a hand, and he took it.

"What did you see up there, Martin dear?" I asked, because I didn't want him to feel alone.

Zach's body tensed beneath me.

"Oh," Marty said. "Just snow."

This was Polo Club's last night together.

AWAY WE-MAIL

From: **Donovan, Deidre**
<dld@westing.edu>
Date: **Wed, Jan 17, at 9:27 AM**
Subject: **Crime Alert - North Wall Vandalism**
To: **ps-all@lists.awaywe-mail.edu**

Dear Students,

On Wednesday, January 17, at approximately 2:35 a.m., a group of six Westing students were caught on camera attempting to vandalize a section of the north-side wall. The students involved in the incident are wanted for questioning. If you have any information about their identity, please contact the undersigned or call Officer Skorzewski at 802-08-20.

If you observe anyone acting in a suspicious or threatening manner, call the Emergency Response Service by dialing 000 immediately. Remember that security measures are in place for the safety of all students.

Deidre Donovan
Director of Investigations
Department of Campus Safety
Westing Academy
Galloway Hall, 117
*802-08-11

SIX MONTHS BEFORE THE CATACLYSMIC, FIERY, KIND OF CLICHÉD END OF ALL THINGS (OR NOT)

TO DIE WILL BE AN AWFULLY GREAT ADVENTURE

The snow melted, and Zach officially changed his AwayWeGo relationship status to "In a relationship with Addie Myers."

The campus matched my mood. The flowers hadn't bloomed yet, leaving rolling grounds full of grays and browns, bare-limbed trees and dead leaves preserved by the cold, a perfect setting for the wave of suicides that broke out in early March, eight in one week. The last of them had been Morgan, president of the Believers. Somehow she'd gotten hold of a bottle of sleeping pills.

So much for *The End Time Is Your Time*.

That didn't stop the Believers, though.

They had a new president now, and more members. They waited in the academic quad, by the library, the cafeteria, ambushing students with flyers, pins, posing questions like, "Have you ever felt empty inside? Like your life is missing something? Like you needed a direction?" I had been accosted no less than three times, and now I was trying to relax, to concentrate on the ducks gliding across the surface of the lake, but Juan wasn't making that easy. Our reflections in the water reminded me of how much taller he was. Instead of Zach and Polo Club I now had Juan and Marty's play. Today the director had called in sick, so Juan, as assistant director, had assumed the role of hounding me. After rehearsal, he insisted we meet up, the two of us, to work on a scene, "a line, if we're being specific, yeah?" he said with a sly grin. He waved his bag of Doritos under my nose and implored me to "consider Darwin's ducks." To "think about Darwin's ducks for a minute or a second or whatever."

I liked to watch the ducks, to feed them bread crumbs, even though we weren't supposed to. Most of all I liked that they could fly over the walls if they wanted, find ducks other than the ones they were stuck with, fall in and out and in of duck love like normal ducks leading normal duck lives.

"Finches," I said between chips.

"Huh?"

"Darwin's *finches*."

"Finches, he says. Whatever, I say. Same point, I say. Strong, most well-adapted survive, weak die. Sure as shit we have *ethics*, right, yeah, I got you, but ethics is a choice, you know? Lots of people, they're not so positive on that choice. Take this on a, umm, fundamental level, Hobbesian natural state of man, zero social contracts, none of that fucking John Locke shit, and we're the exactly same as the ducks."

I was about to correct him again, but he beat me to it. "Finches. Finches finches finches. Fuck's a *finch*, anyway, you get me?"

"We're not *exactly* like them," I said. "We waddle less, for one. And—look at that brown and white one." I pointed. "I'm not *nearly* that good at swimming."

Juan had the uncanny ability to completely ignore anything you said that he deemed irrelevant. As a result, he made no response whatsoever to 95 percent of what came out of my mouth. So I gave him what he was waiting for. I focused on a duckling trailing his mother and tried the last line of the play again.

"To die will be an awfully great adventure."

The look on his face told me everything I needed to know about the successfulness of my attempt. He gestured for me to move closer, but I stayed where I was, so he took a step toward me.

"What I said that night, yeah yeah?" he said, and I could almost feel his hands on my throat again. "Everyone can be killed by someone, no reason, they just fucking snap, like in Camus's *The Stranger*, because it's bright and hot as the devil's nutsack out or something, right? You got me? Well, Peter Pan gets up there and it's, like, an existentialist fuck you to death." Juan raised two middle fingers to the sky, in the direction of God, I guessed. "Peter Pan's like, you got nothing on me, right? I was born to die."

He touched a hand to my wrist, so gently it hurt.

I searched Juan's eyes—long and gray. He was almost twenty and healthy, a breed more mythical than unicorns here at Westing. Is that why he cared so much about this one stupid line? Because any moment his luck was bound to run out?

"You never text me back," he said.

I tried to pull my arm away and he let me.

"I don't know," I said.

"Well," he said simply, and I waited for him to go on and on, the usual, but he says, simply, "I've missed you and your lame-ass Kierkegaardian irony."

I could minimize the hurt.

But maybe he alone wouldn't die.

Maybe I could love him, and he could love me, and I wouldn't have to lose him.

It was a nice thought, so I reached for another Dorito.

I didn't care about rehearsals.

The other actors.

Director, producer, assistant this, lighting that, prop manager.

It was all a blur, a distraction.

I didn't need props.

I didn't even need other people.

Only words, Marty's words.

You could build anything out of words.

They had a *weight* to them.

For the first time, I knew which story was the right one.

Acting was a misnomer. Rather, Noah was the act, and Peter Pan was real. Time bent, compressed, in the weeks leading up to our late-April premiere. The play twisted into my life and my life twisted into the play, as I went over my lines again and again, until they imprinted themselves in me.

While my body sat in my American Revolution classroom listening to how the Battle of Saratoga was the turning point in the war, in my head, I was Peter Pan, in my hospital room with Wendy at my side, flipping through *Game Informer* issues together:

I flipped through Game Informer *issues with Wendy, pretending not to notice as James, a ten-year-old kid in the quarantine ward along with us, was wheeled away by the doctors through a door on stage left, into a section of the hospital from which children did not emerge while soldiers stood guard over the EXIT on stage right. The doctor, the soldiers, all the adults who passed freely in and out of the building wore masks that rendered them indistinguishable from one another. Only the children had faces.*

While my lips pressed against Alice's for the first time in the Galloway gardens and asked her to be my girlfriend, in my head, I was Peter, discussing with Wendy the merits of an unreleased video game called *Spec Ops: Absolution*:

"Spec Ops: Absolution *has a level where you infiltrate a theater as a bartender and get these terrorists who've taken it hostage drunk* so you can take them out one by one by when they go to puke in the bathroom," I said.

"You're lying," Wendy said, rolling her eyes. "No video game yet made is that awesome."

"It is too that awesome," I said, defensive.

Later, we found a message from James hidden in one of the Game Informer issues.

In this reelly cool game Escape from Quantico
your this classless who discovors classless
are disappearing an its becuz the Triumvirate
no the classless have speshul powers.
An I was thinking were like the classless.

"Cool story, bro," I said, to hide the fact that I believed James a little.

Wendy punched me in the shoulder.

"Ow!"

Standing in line in the cafeteria waiting for a sandwich I knew I would hate, I was Peter, pulling a blanket over my and Wendy's heads, spilling Skittles into her hands:

I pulled a blanket over our heads, spilled Skittles into her hands.

"Let's fight the Triumvirate," I said.

"Cool story, bro," she said.

"It's two thirty-three," I said, as if to counter.

"Well, when you put it that way."

The next night at two thirty-three in the morning we became superheroes, battling the League of Tyranny in cities ranging from Tokyo to Madrid. The night after that, we were explorers who'd discovered a new continent, populated by a hostile race of lizard people. Wendy didn't mention my deteriorating vision, that I'd begun stumbling into furniture, and I didn't mention her graying hair, the bald patches that had appeared in several spots on her head.

Afterward, she scrunched her face. "Lizard people? That's like a bad sci fi movie. What were we thinking?"

"Bad sci fi movies are the best movies," I said, with great seriousness.

Again and again, we escaped into other worlds, all of which, we decided, were part of a universe called:

"The Other-verse," I proposed.

"That's dumb," Wendy decided.

"The Vortex?"

"Dumb."

"The Corridor of Doors to Really Cool Worlds."

"Oh my God," Wendy said. "Stop talking." She shoved some Skittles into my mouth, and I laughed, pulled the blanket tighter over the two of us. By the end of the night we settled on Neverland, standing in for all places we could never go.

During a party in which I made out with three boys and one androgynous girl who had close-cropped hair and a firm grip that left red marks on my chin, I was Peter, sitting on an examination room table, waiting for my diagnosis:

I sat on an examination room table with my shirt off as a doctor with a mechanical voice intoned, "There's no easy way to say this, Peter. But it would be best for you to prepare yourself for the likelihood of losing your vision. It might also be time to consider a transfer to a different section of the hospital. A section for more, ah, advanced cases."

The day after the party, when Alice broke up with me and I punched a wall out of self-loathing, I was Peter, and the whole stage had fallen into shadow, all except for me, sitting half naked on the examination table:

182

I sat half naked on the examination table, spot lit, feeling the cold weight of the doctor's diagnosis.

For half a minute, I did not move.

Eventually, the lights dimmed, and I, too, fell into shadow.

The day Alice and I made up, when I bought Alice a cupcake on which the icing spelled SRY and she ate the S and R, leaving a cupcake that demanded "Y," I was Peter, and the stage had lit up for the play's final scene:

I whispered into Wendy's ear that I wanted to go to Neverland forever.

"Don't say that," she said.

"I do," I maintained. "They're going to take me away. They told me."

She understood.

"Peter," she said.

My name, just my name, nothing else.

I couldn't eat for a day and a half before opening night, it made me weak, but it was also reassuring, because feeling pain was better than feeling empty. I wandered the campus in a daze, and as I did, I was Peter, leaning forward, touching my forehead to Wendy's, my way of saying good-bye before rising from my hospital bed to depart to Neverland:

I rose from my hospital bed, and she rose, too, but she was confused. I took a step outside our room, into the corridor, toward the guards and she understood now, I could see her struggling with herself, "I can go alone," I said, and she punched me, "Don't be stupid, Peter," her hand fit neatly into mine, and she pulled me toward the guards with their guns, standing between us and all the places we would never get to go. We ran toward the soldiers, toward the door that we knew led outside, and the soldiers drew their weapons, but we were under our blanket, under the cover of Neverland, we had eaten Skittles in the night and touched forehead to forehead, they couldn't stop us, the soldiers took aim and this was when I said my line: "To die will be an awfully great adventure."

And then everything went dark.

In that darkness, Skittles pattered onto the floor.

The time on the wall read 2:33 in the morning.

The play got a standing ovation, but as I took my bow I was Noah again; that felt like the real tragedy.

That night, everyone who worked on the play, everyone except Marty, got together in Juan's lakeside apartment.

Juan uncorked a bottle of champagne, met my eye, and, saluting me with the bottle, said, "To great adventures."

"To great adventures!" a girl named Lizzie cried; I didn't know what her contribution to the play had been. In fact, I barely knew any of the people who kept clapping me on the shoulder, smiling at me. A guy with puffy sideburns said, "Do you need some crutches?"

"Huh?"

"Because you totally broke a leg out there, man."

Juan circled the room, refilling glasses, refilling my glass. Once the champagne was gone, people began to disperse— Friday night: parties, dances, places to go, no time to linger, no time to dawdle—until only Juan and I were left. He hugged me. He smelled like salt, his shirt was wet. He spoke in my ear. "That line, Noah. Fucking finches, yeah? You nailed the shit out of it."

"Oh, I know."

He rolled his eyes. "Come out tonight, Noah. Let's celebrate. Let me be your Wendy. Say yes. Just say yes. Yes yes yes yes yes."

That's when I noticed he was trembling.

"Are you okay?" I asked. He seemed off—in a rush, somehow,

though we had nowhere to rush to. It was still fairly early, only midnight.

"Fantastic, if you say yes. Don't be difficult, Noah. It doesn't have to be difficult. Just say yes, yeah?"

I guess I nodded, because he kissed me on the cheek and went off to change. I lowered myself into an armchair in his living room to wait. He returned a few minutes later in a new T-shirt, ruffled my hair, and said, "Come on." We traveled through the Friday night together, the sounds of partying all around—laughter and AwayWeTune music tumbling out of windows and from beyond closed doors. Groups of students hurried by, whistled at Juan's arm around my waist. We found our way to the residential quad, glowing in the lamplight, then to a suite belonging to some friends of Juan in Turner House. The door opened, revealing a press of people packed in the common room, everyone talking, smoke trailing from cigarettes and spliffs. A guy next to me raised a shot glass and made an unheard toast. A girl flicked him in the ear and he spilled some alcohol on his pants, flicked her back.

I stepped over a beer bottle laying on the floor, a girl stretched next to the beer bottle, gazing up not *at* the ceiling, but past it. Juan leaned in. "I'll find the alcohol."

I wormed my way into a corner and waited for him to return.

The flicking had been foreplay—the flickers had moved on to dry humping. The boy's long hair kept falling into his face. The girl brushed it back. Brushed it back. I imagined her hand was mine—

A tap on the shoulder.

Juan. No alcohol in hand. He nodded his head in the direction of a hallway. He led me to a door, on the other side of which, we were, quite suddenly, alone, the party muted, though not drowned out. On the nightstand next to the bed stood a bottle of wine, mostly full.

"Didn't know it would be so crazy," he said, massaging the back of his neck. "Few people, she says. Few people. Some close friends, intimate setting, haven't-seen-you-in-forever-my-lovely, whatever and whatever, right? So I'm like yeah yeah let's do it, my lovely was a nice touch, and she says thank you kindly sir, nice, all so nice, except I get here and she's intimate with the toilet, throws a plunger at me and yells at me to go get Derek. Fuck is Derek? And the *music* they're listening to—right? *Right?*"

"The Farsiders, I think."

This answer was too much for him, for he immediately took a long swig from the bottle of wine, then handed it to me. Glancing at the bottle, I said, "I have a policy of not drinking anything that's less than eighty proof."

"Tasting what you're drinking is frightful shit, yeah?"

"Vodka has a taste," I insisted.

"Oh?"

"Fire," I said, fidgeting, unsure of being in someone else's room.

"Look," he said, sensing I was uncomfortable, "My friend, she doesn't mind. I thought—"

"It's okay." I raised the bottle to my lips and took a sip or seven.

We passed the bottle back and forth, until he stopped, studied me very seriously. "Noah. *Noah.* What are we *doing* here?" The wine was nearly gone.

"You dragged me here—"

"No, Noah, *no.* Existentially, right? *What are we doing here?*"

"Existing?" I suggested.

"Existing, he says. *Existing!* Burden of freedom, no reason for anything, yeah yeah? Postmodern relativity of fucking meaning, no grand narratives, not one! *Existing*. Wittgenstein says some things can't be spoken of, so we should shut the fuck up and live, but how can we live if we're going to die?"

He looked at me expectantly, as if I knew anything about Wittgenstein, or living, or dying.

"Vodka helps," I offered.

"I'm dying, Noah," he said. "Bloodwork came in and apparently, *ha,* so that's that, capiche, kaput, finito, I asked for a few more days, okay. They're not all soulless as the devil's cock. They gave it to me. A few more days, before they cart me off. So I could see the play. And do this." He leaned in, and kissed me. He pushed himself into me, onto me, pushed me down on the bed. I tried to press against him, to shift away, but he moved with me, breathed with me, and even as I tried to stop him I pulled him closer, tighter, my fingers tracing the outline of his ribs, his back, until he took his shirt off so I could trace better.

"I can't, Juan," I said. If my body—my chapped lips, the skin peeling on my shoulders, my nose—was the wrong body for Zach, it would be the wrong body for anyone. I heard my fly unzip. I felt Juan's hand. He pulled me close, pressed my head to his chest, and I held on to him, and he held on to me. God, that felt good. I thrust against his hand. He said, "Do you want to stop?" He kept repeating it. "Do you want to stop? Do you want me to stop?" Until finally I said, "No."

Zach didn't want me but at least I had this, whatever *this* was, it felt nice, it felt real, as much as I liked Alice, it felt better than anything we'd done. I came. He spoke softly into my ear, "My turn." He flipped me over, a little roughly, stomach down onto the bed. I heard him take off his shorts.

"*Juan*—" Before I could say more, he was on top of me, *in* me, his hands tight on my shoulders, so tight it hurt. I moaned at first, then I cried out. He held me in place, rooted. I couldn't move, couldn't stop him even if I wanted to; I wasn't sure whether I wanted to stop him or not, and then somehow his hands were on my neck, my throat, he wasn't squeezing but I couldn't breathe. I imagined falling, hurtling toward the ground so fast I couldn't take in air. Would I ejaculate upon impact?

He collapsed onto me as he finished. I breathed. Raising myself up on one elbow, I tried to get up. He wrapped his arms around me.

"Please. Don't go."

I tried to get up again, he wouldn't let me, he said, "I'm sorry"; he said, "I didn't mean to hurt you." He pulled me back, gently, but against my will. He said, "I'm dying. I'm dying. I'm dying. I wanted you to care, okay?"

I didn't answer. His whole body trembled, and I trembled with him.

He said, "I love you."

He said, "I'll do you again, yeah?"

I felt numb; I felt like I might wink out.

He said, "I'm going to blow you, yeah?" but I couldn't get hard. He kept saying he was sorry, he cried into my peeling, disappearing shoulder. He mumbled words into the side of my neck. I waited for him to fall asleep, and then I left.

I never saw him again.

COSMIC SKITTLES
ATOP SUNSET HILL

The week after the play's premiere and Juan's curtain call, Marty dragged me to Sunset Hill at 2 a.m. to see a meteor shower. His attempt at cheering me up. I couldn't say no. We'd been drinking heavily in preparation, while listening to an audiobook on AwayWeRead, in which the main character, Leanna, discovers that she is a robotic surrogate child, and that all her memories are those of the dead daughter she was custom-built to replace. On our way out of Clover House I asked Marty, "How do you know you're real? Or if your love is real?" I leaned into him and he leaned into me. I wrapped my arms around him and let him carry me forward until he said, "Christ, Noah, do some shuffling."

"What?"

"Shuffle."

"That's not the answer I was looking for, Marty."

"Oh," he said, a note of despair in his voice. "I *know*."

We paused by the Wellness Center, the parking lot empty except for the handful of cars belonging to Westing's overnight personnel. I'd misplaced our bottle of scotch somewhere—this upset me so much I'd kicked Clover. Now I was walking with a slight limp.

"*Wellness,*" I said. "What a joke."

"You don't love Alice, do you?"

I looked at him with wide eyes.

"You don't, do you?"

"I love *you*, Marty-guy," I said. "I'm going to ride you around our room like I'm Teddy Roosevelt in the Spanish-American War and you're the horse that got shot out from under me, but from *before* you got shot out from under me, which is why I'm riding you like yippee-ka-yay!"

"Noah."

"Yes."

He didn't continue, so I nudged him in the shoulder. "Don't go all silent on me, not after all we've been through. Those damn Spaniards, messing with our Cuba."

"*Their* Cuba."

"Messing with their Cuba."

"It's—" He went quiet. "I don't want to hurt your feelings, but that was the worst sexual innuendo I ever heard."

"Says the guy who tried to get in my pants by complimenting my nose."

Marty laughed.

It proved surprisingly difficult to get up Sunset Hill when your BAC caused the ground to lurch beneath your feet. Marty stumbled, fell. Before I quite knew what I was doing, I had reached down and picked him up, was carrying him up the hill, step by step, screaming, "Never leave a man behind!"

Marty laughed again and held on to me.

I almost didn't make it to the top. Several times I lost my balance. He didn't tell me to stop, to put him down. He understood I needed to do this for him. I wanted him to know that if he'd been born a slave in the City of Light, I would've carried him out of the darkness, no matter what the Elders did, no matter how many Peacekeepers stood in my way. But there were no great battles at Westing. We had security clacking in the night, long lamp-lit walls equipped with flashing-red cameras, going away silently and appearing as a name under TODAY'S DEPARTEES. We had The Great Cliché with its one-in-ten-thousand chance of impacting Earth on September 26th at 11:37 p.m. We were left to drunkenly climb a hill in the predawn hours with a friend in our arms for no other reason than we felt like picking him up.

"I never thanked you for your play," I said. "Your words," I corrected. "For letting me borrow them."

"I'm waiting."

"That was it, Marty-guy."

"Noah, you don't thank someone by pointing out the fact that you haven't thanked them. That's like saying you read a book by pointing out that you haven't, that you—"

"Thank you, Marty," I said.

He went silent for a time. "I wanted to write something *holy*," he said eventually. "Alice was teaching me the constellations the other day," he went on. "You know all the constellations? Orion and Cepheus and Hercules and Lyra—"

"No," I said.

"They're these old myths, these old holy things," he said. "A religion written in stars. It's beautiful. But why can't we have a new religion? Why can't we have Peter instead of Orion? Why can't we have Wendy instead of Cepheus? That's what I wanted."

I paused, halfway up the hill. We looked up at the sky and he pointed out Peter to me, Peter and Wendy holding hands, and maybe it was the alcohol but I *saw* them standing out against the night, and it was the most beautiful thing, a new constellation that hadn't existed before, until Marty and I played connect-the-dots with the stars, but now it was there, a new myth that we could both believe in; I wanted to shout our discovery from the top of Sunset Hill so all of Westing could crane their heads up and see.

"The meteor shower will be the Skittles," he said.

Marty-guy had given me something beautiful to believe in, and I wanted to return the favor, so I started to tell him a holy thing I knew: "In this book, *The City of Light* . . ." I knew Marty was rolling his eyes—L. J. Sawyer was no Turgenev—but I kept going. "There's this slave who tells Winston about a reeducation camp for rebellious slaves."

"Uh-huh," Marty said, and let loose a tremendous fart. The kind that blows your hair back, if you're the unlucky sap who happens to be carrying the flatulent friend in question up a hill. A second fart followed the first. We were shaking with laughter. Somehow, we ended up side by side on the grass, tears streaming down our faces.

"I'm—gassy—on Tuesday nights," Marty gasped.

"Only—*Tuesdays*?"

"Taco Tuesdays," he explained.

"You could've—warned me," I said, blinking away the tears. Then, "We're going to try this again. No more gas attacks."

"I don't promise anything."

Once I'd gathered Marty up again, I resumed my story. "The reeducation camp I was telling you about? Remember? From before you nearly killed me."

"It was *harmless*."

"That's what they said about zeppelins, and look what happened."

"You're comparing me to the *Hindenburg*?"

I decided not to press the analogy, and instead continued with the story. "The slave said there was this pit that used to be a swimming pool, but the Peacekeepers drained it and used it for—well, they'd randomly pick out a few prisoners, throw them into the pit, give them clubs and sticks, and tell them to kill each other. The last slave standing got to live."

We'd reached the crest. I was still holding him, and he felt so light. That's the only reason I made it. He was so goddamn light, too light for a fight to the death.

"Marty," I said.

"Yeah?"

"You need to eat more. More tacos. You're, like, twenty pounds."

"You're telling me *I* need to eat more?"

I almost dropped him, but held on.

"I just need to believe we wouldn't bludgeon each other to death, because we're best friends even though maybe you hate me a little or a lot."

"I don't hate you," he said quietly. "Why would you say that?"

"You think I don't know?" I asked. Then, "I can break up with her if you want."

"No," he said, and shook his head.

I was still holding him.

I wanted to hold him as long as I possibly could.

The Peacekeepers were going to shoot him if I dropped him. I would have to hold him until the meteor shower, until Peter and Wendy spilled their cosmic Skittles against the sky. Only then could I save him. Only then could we escape to Neverland together.

"Christ, Noah," he said quietly. "I just wish things were different."

I hugged him tighter.

"Because look," he said, holding on to me, "I've been thinking about how it's this crazy thing that we're here, but we forget about how holy it is. It's hard to remember sometimes that Skittles are just as sacred as the Bible if you're sharing them with Wendy and that a blanket can be all the cathedral you need. That's why you need to know what to look for when you look up at the sky."

193

I adjusted my grip on Marty. My arms ached, shook.

"Noah, maybe you should—"

"I want to believe in something, but I don't know if I can. I want a story to believe in, but there are too many to choose from. If I knew what to believe in, I'd be real. I don't feel real. I feel vague, wispy. You know how your breath fogs in the cold and then disappears?"

I couldn't hold him any longer. I would have to put him down. The Peacekeepers would prevail. The soldiers guarding the hospital exit would win.

I had to let him drop, but I did so as gently as I could.

Marty stretched out on the lawn, hands behind his head, while I remained standing, waiting for the meteor shower to begin.

"You ever—you know—thought about—making a run for it?" he asked. "Up and over the wall?"

I waited a few seconds before answering. "You've been reading too many of those F.L.Y. newsletters, Marty." He knew better than me that we wouldn't survive out there. Regular treatment was the only thing keeping him from going blind. "You stayed up there a long time, that night. On the wall."

"Do you think they moved them? The ladders?"

"I don't know," I said.

"If Apep's coming it wouldn't even matter. Whether we're here or out there."

"But Marty-guy, you know better than that. One in ten thousand."

He hesitated. "According to AwayWeKnow. I wonder how much Westing pays them."

I sighed, didn't answer.

That's when the Skittles began to spill across the sky.

THE LAST DAYS BEFORE THE CATACLYSMIC, FIERY, KIND OF CLICHÉD END OF ALL THINGS (OR NOT)

MOTOR CONTROL IS THE FIRST TO GO

The last days before Apep are the kind of hot that makes your clothes stick to your body while sweat runs rivulets across your skin. One afternoon, I return from an orientation leader meeting to find Alice sprawled at the bottom of the stairs, her leg bent at an unnatural angle.

"Thanks for carrying me." She keeps saying that. "Thanks for carrying me." I deposit her as lightly as I can on the sofa, give her a quick kiss. She brushes a hand through my hair. "You're all wet," she says, and I think of Zach, his quest for pneumonia.

I call the Wellness Center from our kitchen phone. They redirect me to EMS. The EMS operator lady speaks in soft tones, assuring me someone will be right over.

"Did you call EMS?" Alice asks from the living room.

"No. I called the petting zoo. They're sending a goat." The joke is automatic, out of my mouth before I can stop to think.

I stay in the kitchen with the phone to my ear, listening to the dial tone, until I hear a knock on the door. They carry Alice out, into the EMS van.

I rest my hand against the back of the idling truck, the metal hot to the touch. I'm about to climb in when an emergency worker shakes his head.

"Sorry," he says, and gives me a sympathetic smile before shutting the door in my face.

I walk.

Down toward the residential quad, where I circle the dorms:

197

Dorlan, Violet, Turner, Clover; Dorlan, Violet, Turner, Clover; Dorlan, Violet, Turner, Clover . . . The Wellness Center's glass facade rises up from beyond the residential quad, brilliant in the afternoon sun.

I approach Wellness. Twenty feet away from its sliding glass doors I turn around and go for a run. Because I'm a shit friend, boyfriend, human.

I circle the campus until my body burns and my breathing comes in gasps. Caloric expenditure has exceeded caloric intake, leading to a caloric deficit, and my body is protesting, responding with austerity measures like the cramp in my side.

Then it all changes. My aching body and labored breathing sink into the periphery. I push myself harder and am aware of the ground beneath my feet, the flowers wilting in the heat on the sides of the trail, the beads of sweat lining my nose, the squirrel a dozen yards away, a bird chirping in the trees. For a moment, I forget about Alice in the EMS van and my unanswered letter to Zach.

Motor control is usually the first to go—the first sign of tertiary stage.

I must keep running.

Alice's doctor is white robed and solemn. In the hallway outside her door, he gives me his best attempt at a comforting expression, which comes out as a grimace. His lips move; I'm listening and I'm not listening: They can't say anything for sure yet, but her blood work is fine. It is, however, very important that I keep an eye on her. The weekly checkups will continue, and in the meantime, if she has difficulty moving her limbs, difficulty talking or breathing, impaired eyesight or hearing, any of the tertiary stage symptoms, they need to know.

"Death is a tertiary stage symptom," I say.

The doctor coughs, a smile frozen on his face. When he turns to leave, I enter Alice's room, shutting the door behind me. She takes my hand in hers. I raise her hand to my lips, suck on her pinky.

"That tickles," she says, laughing. She tries to pull away, but I hold on. Can I finally be decent to her now?

"You have to be more careful," I say.

"What's a broken ankle or two?" She pats the bed next to her, so I sit. She leans her head against my shoulder. "I'm okay, Noah Falls. *Really*. You're the one I worry about."

"Of that I have no doubt."

I lie down beside her.

"Tell me something," I say, still holding her pinky to my lips. So she does.

"There were these summer days, hotter than today, and we would play under the sprinklers to stay cool. There was this boy, Richard, who had a golden retriever. Did I ever tell you about him?"

"The golden retriever?"

"Richard," she says, pretending to be cross. "He had a pool."

"The golden retriever?"

She nudges me gently in the ribs.

"Abuse," I say softly.

"He would invite everyone from the neighborhood, but sometimes sprinklers were just as fun. I liked chasing the boys, their bare backs, skipping stones by the pond, marshmallows and scary stories at campfires. I went to all my brother's Boy Scout things."

"You were a *Boy Scout*?" I asked, laughing.

"Yes," she says with a shrug. "An honorary one. Do you know any scary stories, Noah?"

I thought about it. "One time my girlfriend made me go to chapel services with her—"

Alice elbows me again.

"So much domestic abuse!"

"You're a troll."

"You've *got* to stop calling me that, Alice Witaker."

"Only when you stop trolling, Noah Falls."

"Okay, I've got a story." I hesitate, gathering my thoughts.

"Well? Don't keep me waiting."

"Sorry, your highness," I say. "Once upon a time. . ." The way we're lying together now, how fragile she is, it reminds me of lying on Sunset Hill with Marty, watching comets streak through the sky and believing in constellations of our own making. "Once upon a time there was a boy—or a girl, if you like; it doesn't really matter—so good and decent that everyone knew he wouldn't make it. Sure, we've evolved to have some kindness, some empathy, but too much empathy, too much kindness, that's a liability. Everyone knows that."

"This is a very *Noah* story, isn't it?"

I clear my throat. "So one day while helping a grandma cross the road he got run over by a tractor-trailer."

I pause for dramatic effect, perhaps for a little too long, and Alice withdraws her pinky. "Is that *it*?"

"No!" I exclaim. "So he dies and finds himself face-to-face with God. And God's like, 'Bro. You're an idiot. You got run over by a tractor-trailer while still in the flower of your youth. Who does that, bro?'"

"If you'd gone to chapel with me, you'd know He doesn't sound like that."

I don't let her throw me off. "'However,' God says, 'in spite of your silliness, you're a nice bloke. In fact'—here God takes out a list, down which he runs his omnipotent index finger—'in fact, if you must know, you're the fifteenth nicest bloke in the history of the world. And seven of those guys haven't even been born yet. So, as a reward I'ma grant you any wish you want. Seventy-five virgins? *Done.* A nineteen seventy-six Camaro? *Done*—and if I do say so myself, that would be a fantastic choice. Hell, I can even give you a voice like Melissa Etheridge if you want. You'll be a sensation up here. Lots of Melissa Etheridge fans. We call her Melizzie.'

"And the kid says, 'What about immortality?'

"And God says, 'I recommend going with the Melizzie voice.'

"The kid insists: 'Immortality.' Because he likes people, likes being around them, how they smile with their eyes and whatnot, and he wants to be around them forever, or at least till death by meteor.'"

"This *is* a very Noah story," she says, so I turn my attention toward the end of the bed, our feet inches apart.

"God is true to his word. The kid lives forever. But while he stays young, he grows old inside. Old and tired. He starts to notice little things he never noticed before. Like how, in the year twenty-one fifty, on average, only two out of five people will thank you for holding the door open for them. Little things like that. So one day he stops holding doors open. He stops holding his friends up because you can't hold them forever, stops writing love letters, because they won't be answered anyway. Soon enough, these little things, they add up until the moment comes when he realizes he is no longer happy. So he lives on, unhappy and immortal and no longer the fifteenth most decent bloke in the history of the world, forever."

"Noah." She blows a strand of her out of her eyes. "Your bedside manner is to die for."

"Oh shit," I say, and raise my hand in a high five.

She flicks me in the ear and I laugh. "You know I don't like coarse language."

"Did Richard never use coarse language?"

"A little. He was kind of a bad boy."

My eyebrows arc up in surprise. "Was he now?"

She nods. "Mhm. One time he tried to steal a TV from a classroom. All the girls were crazy about him."

"Naturally." A couple seconds pass. "Alice?"

"Another story?" she asks, feigning wariness.

"Not exactly." I swallow, stare up at the ceiling. "I know this—it doesn't justify it or—but I want you to know. I want to *say* it. It has nothing to do with you. The whole thing with Zach. You're the best."

She bites her lip, nods, and in the silence that falls over us, enclosed by the sterile white walls of the room, we pretend that being the best has ever been enough for anyone.

We move Alice downstairs, into the living room. She's terribly awkward on her crutches, but categorically refuses to use her wheelchair, prefers jumping on one foot as a means of locomotion when she absolutely has to get from one place to another, hair flying in all directions, cold determination set into her soft face. Marty is always with her, fetching her juice and snacks, changing the sheets, sitting by her side. Once I saw them holding hands and my breath caught a bit.

A week after her fall, I attempt to check her temperature before running off to bring some dinner back to the apartment before the cafeteria closes. Marty's meeting me there.

"I'm fine, Noah. Really. Twice a day—it's a teeny bit overkill, isn't it?"

"Just be thankful it's an oral thermometer."

Somehow this is what our relationship has come to. *Hey, honey. You're not dead yet, are you? Okay, good.*

"Will you cook something for me sometime?" she asks from

the sofa. She looks up from this year's orientation packet, which she's been reading in preparation for welcoming the newsies when they arrive next week. "Not now, I mean—sometime. You seem to like it. Cooking."

"Still trying to improve me, I see."

"You know what they say about old habits."

"They're annoying as hell?"

She smiles.

"I'm only good at scrambled eggs," I warn. "Anything else is hit or miss. Mostly miss."

"That's okay."

"Tomorrow, then," I say. "Prepare to have your mind blown."

When I get to the cafeteria Marty's already there, wandering from station to station with this blank look on his face. "Oh," he says, upon seeing me. "I'm not sure what I want. Alice said she was craving *pizza*, but I don't really want anything. Maybe a sandwich."

I make a gagging noise to convey my enthusiasm for his choice of nourishment, bump him in the shoulder as I pass. "Well, I'm getting a hot dog." But it bothers me a little, that he knows what Alice wants and I don't.

I'm being unfair, I know.

I hate myself for it.

"It's ironic," he says. "You have this, this vendetta against sandwiches, and a hot dog is just a—"

"Martin dear. Don't you dare say what I think you're going to say."

"It's just a sandwich, isn't it?"

I shake my head. "If I had something to throw at you . . ."

"It's good you're eating, though," he says, with a concerned, motherly look.

"I eat," I protest. "Here and there."

We end up *both* getting hot dogs and I grab a couple slices of pizza for Alice. On our walk back, to prove I'm not upset with Marty, I explain to him the difference, the essential difference, between a hot dog and a sandwich, why one is an acceptable means of sustenance and the other is an abomination packed between sliced bread: "A hot dog is cooked."

"But roast beef is cooked. And bologna. The meat's always cooked. It's not *raw*."

"The meat is warm," I amend.

"So, if you put a sandwich in the microwave—"

"It turns into a hot dog, yes, very good, Martin dear."

We pass behind Galloway, the lake water dark and brooding, the outline of the Lakeside Apartments visible in the falling dusk.

"You know I read on AwayWeKnow a couple weeks ago," he says, "a guy who was on death row, they asked him what he wanted for his last meal and he said a cheeseburger. A McDonald's cheeseburger. Do you remember McDonald's?"

"I remember the toys. They always had those toys. From movies."

"My parents would get me Chicken McNuggets. I miss them."

"The McNuggets?"

He laughs.

At the door to our apartment he asks, "Hey, have you thought at all about joining F.L.Y.? We could use more people. . . ."

"We?" I echo.

He shrugs. "A recent development."

I gesture with my to-go boxes. "Hold this for me?"

"Yeah."

I search for an objection. There are so many, it takes some

time to settle on one. "I don't want to get kicked out of here, Marty. One close call was enough, wasn't it?" I grope in my pockets for my keys. "You haven't told them about the key—" I start, and picture it lying on my nightstand.

"Of course not," he says, reproachful.

I nod, let it go. "Martin dear, it was just a game, wasn't it?"

It comes out patronizing, so I cut myself short, don't tell him he'd go blind before he ever found so much as a McNugget. We drop the subject and eat dinner together on the living room sofa, the three of us. I let Marty and Alice talk. She's telling him about our orientation leader training. When we're done eating, Marty and I wash out the cups and utensils in the kitchen. The hot water is soothing. But Marty's not finished with our earlier conversation.

"If this were a book or a play," he says meaningfully, "wouldn't you want the heroes to do something holy and wondrous?"

"I thought you hated *The City of Light*," I said.

"Like Wendy and Peter," he says, his voice soft. He adjusts his glasses.

"Marty—" I'm about to tell him that in *The City of Light*, Winston and Jena lead the slaves in rebellion against the city's Elders, because Winston and Jena are brave, because Winston and Jena are in love, because Winston and Jena know the city of light is a city of evil. In *Escaping Eternity*, Kylie discovers that the assignment process which determines a citizen's social role in the Eternal State is rigged to keep power in the hands of the powerful, and she teams up with Tristan, the son of the local governor, to escape outside the border fence, to a place where she and Tristan can be whatever they want to be. But what do *we* know? What did Polo Club ever discover?

"You were Peter," he says, biting his lip. "I thought you'd understand."

"Marty," I say, "What does F.L.Y. even want? If you run away, the only thing that'll happen is you'll get eaten by a bear."

"Maybe it doesn't matter if we get eaten by bears, Noah. That's what I learned from writing the play. What matters is—what you do. The act. That's what we have. What Peter and Wendy had."

He watches me as I dry a cup.

"All we do at Westing is make things up," I press. "Maybe aliens infected the world. Maybe it's a punishment from God. Maybe we get downloaded into chips. Maybe they experiment on us like rats. Maybe the stars are Peter and Wendy. Or maybe they're all just stories." I can't stop myself now, so I go on. "Maybe they take us away to tertiary centers and give us incontinence support until we die. Maybe that's it."

A long time passes before he says, "What they did to Melanie was wrong. A place that does that . . ." He hesitates. "A place that does that is worth running away from."

"The baby wouldn't have lived," I say.

He just shakes his head at me.

Through the window, I notice our little apple tree has been shorn from its roots, probably from last night's thunderstorm. Our tree's last apples are scattered across the yard. I push open the screen door and pick them up, one by one. Minutes pass; my arms grow full. Marty comes out to help me. We gather the apples wordlessly as the horizon dims, little by little.

I want to tell him I'm sorry.

But the apples are unwieldly.

I need to concentrate, lest they spill from my grasp.

WORDS, WORDS, WORDS!

The Great Cliché is only three weeks away.

I went for a run this past Friday, jogged past a hundred Believers lying prone on the grass, pretending to be dead, practicing for September 26th I guess, with placards and posters that read "Make the End a New Beginning," and "Suffering Is Punishment for SIN. Repent NOW, and Be Saved." As I jogged, a song I've been listening to nonstop on AwayWeTune played in my head. When I passed Clover House, I heard it cranked to max volume.

Are you going to Scarborough Fair
Remember me to one who lives there
She once was a true love of mine
He's still here.
Tell her to make me a cambric shirt
Without no seams nor needlework
Then she'll be a true love of mine

I haven't visited since I delivered my letter, and he's remained silent, but that's okay, I'm okay.

Tell her to find me an acre of land
Between the salt water and the sea strand
Then she'll be a true love of mine.

I hooked up with a very nice blond boy to prove how okay I was. He had a slim build and small, girlish hands. I sincerely hope to never see him again. Couldn't look at Marty or Alice for days after. Alice, clacking along on her crutches. Giving her newsies a campus tour in that believe-in-me-and-ye-shall-be-saved voice of hers.

I have my own group of newsies, and they keep me busy.

I'm not supposed to have a favorite, so of course I do.

Jane is quiet and sarcastic, likes to joke about her impending death. Rumor has it she is a master AwayWeGamer already; she has one of the top ten Zombie Survival scores. Her corner of the room she shares with Lin and Michelle is meticulous, folders stacked, books in a neat line along the windowsill, dirty laundry disposed of in three bins—one for lights, one for colors, and one for jeans. She's the third wheel in that room, which makes me like her more.

Naturally, I treat her coldly. On her second day she called to tell me she'd lost her keys.

"I think that's it. My brain is going. This is the end."

"Security's in Galloway seventeen, on the ground floor," I said, refusing to play along. "They'll give you another key."

"I'm going to dictate my last will and testament to you," she said.

"I've got to go, actually, but another time."

I hung up, and resumed playing Age of Rome, where my parents have been sending me florins with increasing frequency. Once, my dad showed me a game on his computer, a racing game. I didn't understand why you would need a computer to race when you had a perfectly good toy car. But we raced each other, our hands poised over the keyboard.

The kids help. They keep me busy, and busyness is a temporary remedy for the emptiness that rises in me more and more frequently as autumn's first chill sets in. Westing has all sorts of activities for the newsies, from barbecues to movie nights to alcohol/drug seminars. The night before convocation, I stumble into Allison, one of my newsies, at a room party in

Turner, drunk off her face, talking to a pair of boys much bigger than her, and much more sober.

I consider leaving. *Do* leave. It's hard to exert authority when some of your charges, Allison included, are as old as you. But I pause in the hallway, listening to the music stream out from beneath the door.

What would Zach do?

So I go back for her.

She hugs me. Says, "Noahhhh!" Says, "I missed you!" Says to the two boys, "This is my orientation leader," with this great big smile. They look flustered. I know what they're after, and they know I know.

I say, "Ally, do you want me to take you home?"

"Home? *Home?*" She laughs. "It's only midnight!"

"You don't want to be drifting off during the director's speech tomorrow."

"Oh *please*. You don't actually expect us to go to that, do you?"

Considering I slept through convocation last year, I'm not sure what to say. Before I can figure it out, she grabs my hands. "Stay with us, Noah!"

"Can't. It's—against protocol. I'm not even supposed to be in the same room as you, if you're drinking. I really think you should—" I drop my voice to a whisper. "These guys—"

"I know," she interjects. "I'm drunk but not an—*an idiot*, Noah." She pulls me closer. "Do *you?*"

"I'm leaving," I say. "Do you want me to walk you home?"

She bites her lip. "No."

"All right. Be careful."

I worry about her all the way back to my apartment even though it's ridiculous. Why do I care how many dicks she rides? I guarantee I have her beat, anyway. But the moment I step through the door I see Alice on the couch, wiping angrily at her eyes, her wheelchair in the corner. She tries to hide behind her hands, pretend she hasn't been crying.

I feel like crying with her; maybe that would fix, if not everything, then something, *a* thing.

I want to tell her I don't know what I'm doing, which stories are true and which not, whether the world is ending at 11:37 p.m. on September 26th or not, if PPV is a punishment from God or an infection seeded by a hostile alien race or simply, simply—the cruelest possibility of all—an accident of nature, with no more intrinsic meaning than a sneeze.

I want to tell her I saw her and Marty kissing the other day. She shies away from me, picks up her crutches, pushes herself up from the sofa, and clacks off into the kitchen.

I need a minute or two to swallow my self-loathing. It tastes like vomit. Alice glances up from the kitchen table and sniffs as I enter.

"I'm just—" I let out a sigh. "I'm jealous of you." I pause. "You and your newsies. I'm horrible at it. All of it. That's the truth. And—"

And what? She waits for me to finish the thought. As if I know how.

Words. So many yet never enough!

She snorts then. Through tears and mucus she says, with surprising calm, "Oh, Noah. You're not the only one who has it hard. You think you're the only one who could use a drink?"

I've never seen her like this, speaking like this. "That's not true," I say, without conviction.

"It is, though, Noah Falls. You think you're the only one who's ever been hurt."

"You want a drink?" I reach inside the Cap'n Crunch cereal box on top of the refrigerator, withdraw a bottle of vodka, put it on the table in front of her. "Have a drink. Have a whole bottle. Make a toast."

"Noah—"

"Go on," I say.

"You don't think I will," she says.

She unscrews the cap, brings the bottle to her lips.

I wait for her to do it.

"I could use a drink, Noah Falls." Then she puts it down, and softens. "But it's a crutch. I wish you could see that."

"You have your crutches," I say, nodding at her broken ankle, "I have mine." I scoop the bottle up and take a swig. I hate myself for it, and to drown the hate I take another gulp.

She makes a noise, half laugh, half sob. "Do you know Marty told me something today?"

"No," I say quietly. He must've finally come out with it. Only Alice would cry after breaking someone else's heart.

When she doesn't go on, I prompt her: "What?"

"Never mind," she says, looking away.

"*What?* What is it? He's in love with you? Don't tell me that wasn't obvious."

"I guess," she says, "we're all in love with the wrong person, aren't we?"

We study each other in silence.

"Why have you stayed?" I ask after a time, even though I don't know if she's still "with" me or not. Even though I'm not even sure what it means to be "with" someone, when you can't even touch them, when they're always out of your grasp, when all you do is hurt them or misunderstand them, when you are so full of empty space.

"Because I love you." She says it so simply, so innocently. "Don't tell me that wasn't obvious."

"Don't say that." I sound too harsh, so I add, "I never thought I'd say it. But there's a little too much love in my life at the moment."

She laughs, and I let out the breath I didn't even realize I was holding.

"Well, I'm saying it anyway, Noah Falls. I love you, I love you, I love you, I love you—"

"Don't," I say. My voice sounds pathetic, even to me.

"I know *you*," she says. "I love that you hate sandwiches for some inexplicable reason. I love that you told Martin you preferred Dr. Seuss to Pushkin. I love that you're a bigger troll than everyone else on AwayWeGo combined. I love *you*, Noah. I wish I didn't, but I can't help it. I know you don't love me the way I love you. The way I want you to love me. I know it's selfish. If I weren't selfish, I'd love Marty, but I can't, I told him I can't."

"Today?" I ask, even though she basically just told me a second ago.

"Maybe—" she breaks off. "Maybe if we were out there. If we had billions to choose from. It would be different. But we're here. *Here*. I believe this *matters*. That we're here for a reason. That out of all the billions you and me are here for a reason."

"I don't believe in reasons," I say.

I've never seen someone wipe at her nose so angrily. "How does *Zachary* make you feel?"

I bite my lip. "Half the time I regret meeting him and half the time I think he's the best thing that ever happened to me. It's very unreasonable."

Alice tries to hold back her laugh, but it escapes.

I reach out, touch her hand, hold it. I say, "If you still want me, I won't leave you."

She says, "Okay."

ALCOHOL AWARENESS NIGHT

Fast Facts

Alcohol Use Leads to:

- Impaired judgment, loss of coordination, slowed reflexes, and memory loss

- Weight gain, vomiting, stomach ulcers, and stomach cancer

- Diseases like cirrhosis and hepatitis

- Sexual dysfunction

Reduce Risk of Harm by:

- Abstinence

- If abstinence is not possible, imbibe no more than two standard drinks daily, and no more than four standard drinks on any one occasion

What Is a Standard Drink?

350 mL Beer = 150 mL Wine = 50 mL Hard Alcohol

DREAMS OF SELF, TO BE CONTINUED

Noah looks in the mirror, but does not see himself reflected in it.

He says, "Hand me my mouth."

And there! A mouth appears in the mirror's reflection.

It smiles approvingly at itself.

"Eyes, too, because right now the fact that a mouth can see itself is something of a fantastic conceit. Oh, and a brain would be nice."

And there! Reflected in the mirror are a brain and a pair of eyeballs and a mouth, each floating freely, unconnected to the others. The eyes wander through the air in opposite directions. One knocks over a bottle of deodorant.

He says, "Legs!"

"Arms!"

"Leprosy!"

In this way, little by little, Noah assembles himself.

And there he is! In the full glory of his naked form.

He blinks, and as soon as his eyes flick open, he is back to what he saw in the beginning.

In short: nothing.

In short: empty space.

Again he tries to assemble himself, listing the component parts: "mouth," "eyes," "brain," and on.

Again, he blinks.

Again, his reflection vanishes.

He turns on the shower. When the mirror fogs over, he touches his finger to the glass. In place of his reflection, he begins to write.

He does not know how to write a holy story, so he will have to settle for fiction:

I am Peter Pan.

The words do not disappear.

And suddenly, he can see himself more clearly than he has ever seen himself before. His bathroom is not a bathroom, but a stage, and the auditorium is full of shadowy faces, because life requires witnesses, whether or not they clap or boo, chew loudly or talk on their phones.

But then, a thought occurs: "I don't know any of these people. I can't even make them out. I am not Peter Pan."

The stage disappears, along with the audience.

He is back in the bathroom, in front of an empty mirror.

On a whim, Noah begins to list his real audience: "Zach."

And in the mirror, briefly, Noah recognizes his own face.

To keep himself from disappearing, he continues: "Marty, Alice, Juan, Alex . . ."

He is happy.

He has found the way to create a lasting impression of himself.

But then, a thought occurs: "My friends will die. Other sacks of decaying meat are a precarious foundation for selfhood, no?"

His reflection shrugs, and says, "Your phone is ringing, you existential crybaby. I guess your little project here is to-be-continued?"

Noah is affronted. "You don't have to be rude."

"*Beep*," his reflection says.

CONVOCATION DAY

Beep.

Alice stirs beside me in her bed.

Beep.

Seconds pass.

Beep.

My feet hit the hardwood with a thud. I stumble around Alice's darkened room, searching for the source of the noise.

Beep.

"What is—sound," she mumbles, still half asleep.

The noise is coming from my pants, in a heap on the floor of Alice's room.

"Nothing," I say. "Go to sleep."

The text is from Sarah. . . Allison's roommate. It reads, *Ally is sick and i dont no what to do*

God. Allison and those fucking boys.

"Noah?" Alice says, shifting in the bed.

"I'll be back in a bit."

I text *be right there*, slip my clothes on, stuff the cell in my pocket, push out into the corridor. The door to my room hangs open, so I shut it with a click. I'm about to run down the stairs when I stop myself. Marty's door is a couple feet away. I could apologize, I could pull him into a hug, press our foreheads together and reaffirm our shared mythology. I shouldn't have ever made fun of it. But apologizing is hard, sorting through this tangle of feelings is hard, and besides, one of my kids needs me, the only kids I'll ever have.

I knock anyway, but he doesn't answer.

I don't blame him.

On the path that runs from the apartments to Galloway, I pause, and text him:

lunch tmrrw? u can quote Tolstoy and i wont even groan 2 loudly.

And another: *under 100 decibels, i prmise.*

A few minutes later, he texts back: *thanks for carrying me that one night.*

In Galloway, a girl rides the elevator with me up to the fourth floor; neither of us acknowledges the other. Tomorrow. Marty and I will talk tomorrow. *Tomorrow and tomorrow and tomorrow . . . till the last syllable of recorded time, and all our yesterdays have lighted fools the way to dusty death!* The girl and I avert our eyes, listen to the hum of the elevator. When the doors open we go our separate ways, like shadows fleeing before the light. That or two strangers, tired as all fuck, too tired, even, to entertain similes for more than a second or two.

Inside room 413, Allison has caught the trash can in a trembling embrace. I watch her heave as I silently repeat a mantra that serves me well in such times.

Must keep eyes open. Must keep eyes open. Must—

My gaze drifts across pre-calc textbooks and pink beanbag chairs. Littered across the floor are clothes, pillows, the semester's first copy of the *Westinger*. Her roommate Sarah has a birthmark the shape of Italy on her neck and is dressed in a wispy thin blue night-robe. She looks on with an expression that is simultaneously *very* concerned and *very* unfocused, hair ruffled, long black strands going every which way. She says something I don't catch.

"Sorry?" I say.

"It's her second time," Sarah says blankly, drawing her robe more tightly around her. "Throwing up," she adds, as if I'm blind.

I nod, to show Sarah I understand.

"We had salads."

"Salads," I say, staring at the dangling ends of her robe.

"At dinner," she explains, tucking a loose strand of hair behind her ear. "I had Caesar and she had this vinaigrette thing."

"A vinaigrette," I say.

"I didn't think she ate enough to throw anything up."

"She drank a lot?" I ask, my gaze catching on a pair of empty Poland Spring bottles on the floor.

Sarah opens her mouth, closes it, then opens it again. "It's her second time," she says.

I shake my head. "Sorry, that's not what I—" I cut myself off. "She drank a lot of water?" I gesture to the bottles. "Before bed?"

"I guess. I—don't really know."

"Right," I say. "Right. She probably drank too much water. You can drink too much."

By now, Allison's finished puking. She's slumped next to the trash can.

"Ally, I'm sorry," Sarah starts, and I realize she's apologizing for *me*, for calling *me*.

Allison speaks over her roommate, says, "Feel like shit." She turns to me. "Don't call EMS. Please."

"Okay."

"I've heard Westing mails your parents reports," Allison says. "Can't. Don't want them—"

"Okay," I say.

"I thought I'd be happy," Allison is saying. "Here. Come here and. Be. Happy. But nobody here is happy. I've been here—week and a half, okay?"

218

"Okay," I say.

"Apocalypse cults and everyone's counting down the days. Twelve days. One, two, three, four, five, six, seven, eight, nine, ten, eleven, twelve! And *you're not happy.*" Her voice rises. "*You're* not happy."

She starts to get up. I offer my hand. She brushes past me, collapsing onto her bed.

"On your side," I say, and place the trash can by her bed.

"It *smells.*" She tries to push it away with her foot.

In the bathroom I empty her trash into a larger bin, but there's still puke clinging to the sides of the can. I fill the can up with hot water from the sink just as a guy pushes through the door, heading toward a urinal. When he's done and washing his hands he watches me swish the hot water around and around, trying to get at all the puke. I empty the mucky water into a nearby toilet, repeat the process several times.

"You're a hero," he says to me. His eyes are red. He claps me on the shoulder and repeats, "Hero."

I bring the trash can back to Allison's bedside, where she has fallen asleep. Then I'm in Galloway's tiled halls again. Allison will probably be all right. *Probably.* I pause by a window and take out my phone, dial 000.

"Emergency Response Service, what is your emergency?"

"Galloway room four-one-three, alcohol overdose," I say, and hang up.

But why?

If not tonight, then a week, a month, a year from now.

I'll have to see Allison tomorrow, or rather, *later today,* shepherd her and all the rest of my newsies to the chapel for the director's convocation day speech. She will hate me, but it will be okay, because I can't promise her a week, a month, a year, but I can her promise tomorrow, and tomorrow, and tomorrow.

It's the best I can do, and maybe that's okay.

There are no great battles, no Peacekeepers or Elders to lead a rebellion against, no beautiful slaves to save. But there are small moments, small gestures, like dialing a phone, like directing your newsies to security when they lose their keys, making sure they get to convocation all right, and maybe small gestures can also be great battles. Maybe there are ways to be a hero that do not involve saving whole cities.

If you accumulate enough small moments, you become *real*.

A dozen feet ahead, a boy rounds a corner.

A small coincidence—it is the boy from some nights before, blond haired and slender. He stops in his tracks. We study one another in the quiet. The feeling that it is possible to be a hero swells inside me.

What is a relationship, if not a story? A series of small moments and coincidences that memory strings together into narrative. Narrative that fills the empty space inside us. Narrative that is a hero's weapon against the great tragic powers of the world.

Without a word, I fall into him.

Without a word, he takes my hand and leads me away to his room. The angels can wait their turn.

Autumn light streams through the window. He is golden in it.

The wall clock reads 10:19, which leaves me exactly two hours and forty-one minutes to get myself together, meet Marty for lunch, and shepherd my kids to convocation. If I'm feeling ambitious, I might even have time to check in on Allison to make sure she's alive to hate me.

I linger in bed, trying to figure out what he smells like.

Salt. Sweat. Cum. A whiff of tobacco. We smoked the night

before, sat on the windowsill and passed a cigarette back and forth. His nails were pristine.

Our legs are tangled, and a sliver of his chest pokes out from under the blanket. His foot brushes mine.

"You know," I say, "I think I might be bi-curious."

He snorts softly. "You ruined it. We had that whole silent and mysterious thing going. Was kinda hot."

"Like a nineteen-twenties porno."

He brushes a bit of hair out of his eyes. "You want to—" He pauses.

"Fuck?"

"I was going to suggest food."

"I can't," I say, and tell him the truth, or at least try to. It's easier, with a stranger. "I'm sorry. It's just—I'm dating a girl. But I'm gay and she knows I'm gay. And I'm in love with a guy but he's straight and going to die. Soon. So there you have it."

He raises an eyebrow. "And this prevents you from ingesting food?"

A witty retort fails to present itself, so I pick myself up off the bed and dress. I'm almost to the door when he says, "Hey. Wait."

I turn.

"If this were some sappy AwayWeWatch rom com, I'd ask you if I can at least know your name. But I'm not going to do that."

"'A rose by any other name would smell as sweet,'" I quote.

"That makes us roses, I suppose."

"Me, specifically."

"Tell me one thing."

"Okay."

"What's the beginning of time?"

"What?" I say, more from surprise at the question than curiosity at an answer.

"The letter *T*."

I can't help smiling. "Oh yeah?"

"Yeah."

"I got one for you then. What's the meaning of life?"

"I'm lying down, so go ahead—"

"The condition that distinguishes organisms from inorganic objects and dead organisms, manifested by prodigious quantities of existential angst, alcohol-induced reproduction, and the power of adaptation to the environment with the aid of AwayWeBlog self-help blogs about lessons we can learn from canine companions we haven't had since we were children."

He laughs. "I'm going to tell my friends about you, you know. I'm going to tell them I met a boy and I fucked him once and I fucked him twice and then he told me the meaning of life."

"Hey, now that we've shared the secrets of the universe with each other, want to do me a favor?"

In the shower, I use a bottle of golden boy's bodywash, dry myself off with one of his towels. Couldn't bear to go back to my apartment to clean myself up. Not after Alice and I had that whole talk and then I went and fucked—well—the first golden boy I ran into.

He tells me to leave the bodywash and towel on his bed.

"The sheets will get wet," I say.

"It doesn't matter." He leans in. It is an awkward, almost platonic kiss. We part with the finality of somber "Bye"s and the shutting of a door. The feeling that something inexpressible passed between us hangs over me. And I'm not simply referring to the uncommonly decent caliber of our lovemaking.

It is that rightness I felt earlier.

The sense that I was solid, and full, and real.

222

I try to hold on to this feeling, this warmth, whatever it is, this thing that draws people together, the pull of coincidence and story-making.

My head feels numb. I need to speak to someone. I need to speak to—

Marty.

I need to apologize to Marty, to make things right between us.

I text him: is lunch at 11 ok?

I set off toward the cafeteria half running, not waiting for a response. I push through Galloway's main entrance and almost walk into a campus security cart. There's at least a dozen of them in front of Galloway alone, and for the first time in as long as I can remember, men in blue, with holstered guns. I count four police cruisers parked on the Galloway lawn, even more in the parking lot, lights flashing. We never had this sort of fuss over convocation last year. Then again, I spent most of the day last year tucked into a fetal position, massively hungover, and slipping every now and then into erotic dreams about Alex (all in all, not a bad day) while outside they lit up the sky with fireworks. I hurry toward the cafeteria. Hassled-looking teachers linger on the cafeteria steps with cigarettes pressed to their lips.

I pick a lone table in a distant corner of the caf, flanked on two sides by windows that look out into the direction of the greenhouse. Marty hasn't responded.

I text him Here.

Ten minutes pass. Twenty.

At 11:30 I text, martin dear. u coming or am I goin 2 have 2 endure the caf by my lonesome?

I text, i want 2 talk.

I force a hot dog down my throat, pick at some dead skin on my forearm, wondering if golden boy noticed.

223

Here I am, sitting by myself at lunch, in a crowded cafeteria, picking at flaking pieces of me, wanting to tell my best friend, *what*, what is it that I want to say about the warmth I felt? I feel holy, like the night we created new constellations together—no, *felt*, the sensation has already passed. I felt holy, but what made me feel holy in the first place was a transgression, a stolen moment of warmth with a golden boy, a story that would hurt both Marty and Alice, if I recounted it to them. It seems ridiculous, now, that I thought I had anything to say. Here I am, in a glorified hospice, trying to speak of holiness and love! Love makes us immortal! Love makes us eternal! Oh Zach, give it to me up the ass and I'll see the face of God!

I laugh at myself.

That's when my phone rings.

I pick it up, expecting to hear Marty's voice.

"This is Nurse Sanders, from the Wellness Clinic. Am I speaking to Noah Falls?"

Jane passed out halfway through her morning yoga class.

"During downward dog," she explained, over the phone. "The doctors say I can go to convocation but you need to look after me to make sure I don't give up the ghost."

Outside Wellness, I flip my phone open and group-text my newsies: minor emergency. meet you inside the chapel?

I look up and there's Jane, striding through the sliding glass doors.

"My blood work is fine," she says, by way of introduction. "But if I go into cardiac arrest, you'll have to give me CPR. Can you handle that, Orientation Leader?"

I laugh. "I guess we'll see."

There is a horde of protesting students on the chapel lawn,

large even by Westing standards. Jane and I push through campus security and local police. There are several more police cruisers parked on the grass by the chapel. Inside, news crews have set themselves up near the pulpit at the front, tripods deployed, cameras flashing. Reminds you how big a deal Westing is, how much taxpayer money is going into this experiment, this pilot project of the government's. We're all worth tens of thousands of dollars. A reassuring thought, to have your life valued so highly.

Everywhere I turn, students, faculty, administrators. So many people. Countless signs waving in the air.

"Spread your wings and F.L.Y."

"We Will Be FREE."

"Westing is a CULT. Don't drink the Kool-Aid."

"'Those who surrender freedom for security will not have, nor do they deserve, either one.'—Benjamin Franklin."

The administration likes to stress that a minority of the student body is associated with F.L.Y.; strictly speaking, they're not lying. Fifty-one percent of the students in the hall aren't waving a damn thing.

At the pulpit, the director of Westing and a number of her assistants fiddle with the microphone, filling the stuffy air with unpleasant scratchy noises. My stomach grumbles. At lunch I didn't have much of an appetite. Now I'm packed in here with a legion of newsies, brought in to replace us. I am tired and hungry and there's no sign of the rest of my kids.

"Sorry we have to sit so far in the back because of me," Jane says, brushing a strand of hair behind her ear. "I can imagine how much you were looking forward to this."

"Highlight of my year," I say. "How you feeling?"

"Alive, for now." She grimaces, as if this is a problem she's been meaning to resolve.

"Yeah," I say. "Yeah." I know I should say more. Make another joke. Say something amusing. Clap her on the shoulder. Are guys allowed to clap girls on the shoulder? What would Zach do?

The director saves me from the pressure of being a decent human being.

She adjusts the microphone one last time, and begins:

"By now you've all heard of the incident that took place late last night, at about two-thirty in the morning, in which a number of students from a student organization named the Front for the Liberation of Youths in Recovery attempted to rush the main gate. To put an end to all rumors and speculation, let me say this. The students were caught on camera as they approached the gate. Campus security notified local law enforcement personnel because of the size of the group. As a result of rash and foolhardy actions taken by both sides, a confrontation ensued. Two students were fatally wounded, and an officer is currently at a nearby medical center, where he is being treated for head injuries."

The place is so quiet I can hear Jane breathing beside me.

Only two words, but difficult to process.

Fatally.

Wounded.

"What happened last night is a tragedy not only for those directly affected, but for all of us who have to dwell in the aftermath, and whose solemn duty it is to persevere in the face of renewed criticism of our cause. The question we keep coming back to is: Why are we here? It all circles back to that. Even here, on this very campus, we have heard similar objections and complaints, from teachers and students alike. Why bother with grades and papers, final exams and research projects, art exhibitions and dance recitals? To what end? What good is a student's transcript if we know she will never truly leave

Westing? Never apply for an internship, never go to college, never get a job?

"After all, though we do not speak of it, we all know it. The only place students go after Westing is away to hospice care, to a tertiary care facility twenty minutes' drive from the school, where all our students go when we can no longer provide for them here. But while you are here, we hoped to give you some small fraction of normalcy, of the life you might've lived had you not been infected. While you are here, we hoped you might read Plath and Steinbeck late into the night, study the history of the Qing Dynasty, discover a passion for the workings of the American political system. We hoped you might fall in love with the beauty of a mathematical proof, be filled with wonder at using a telescope to look back in time. We believe education has a human value, is a human right. It has always been our mission to extend that right to you, and in time, to all youths in recovery.

"But we need your help. You must work. You must produce. We believe there are Michelangelos and Sapphos here. Prove us right. Stay within these walls. If not for yourselves, then for all those afflicted youths less fortunate than you, so that they might have a chance to live the lives you live right now."

She pauses to take a sip from a cup offered to her by one of her aides. "I apologize to our newest cohort of students for such a grave introduction to Westing. But given the circumstances . . ." Clearing her throat, she says, "In spite of the difficulties and in the face of skepticism from legislators and media alike, Westing has prospered. You are its future. You are its stewards and its keepers, and it, in turn, will come to be your home. Welcome. Remember not everyone has such a home. Remember all those students of Westing who are no longer with us—especially the two misguided youths we lost last night: Troy Davis Holland and Martin Hugo

Singer. Hold those names in your memories and do not follow in their footsteps, for what happened to them was needless. A true waste. But most of all—most of all, remember why you are here."

For a few long seconds, nobody in the chapel says a word.

Then a chorus of voices erupts:

"What did you really do to Marty and Troy?"

"The administration lies!"

"We won't go to your tertiary death camps!"

"Pass the Kool-Aid!"

I can't breathe. I know I *should* but it's a surprisingly difficult task, the working of my lungs, the contraction and expansion of my chest. Jane asks me something unintelligible, and I do not respond.

Dozens of kids rise from their seats to yell, "Pass the Kool-Aid!" until it grows into a chant.

Cameras flick and flash from every direction.

All I can think about is his middle name was Hugo.

I didn't even know.

Maybe the director is lying.

Maybe Marty escaped into the fields and trees and roofs lit beyond Westing's walls.

It's a story that I want desperately to believe in.

There is a blond-haired girl with a mole on her neck sitting directly in front of me.

I throw up in her hair.

LIFE IS
[INSERT METAPHOR HERE]

There are no celebratory convocation day fireworks tonight.

I sneak onto the library roof and dangle my feet over the edge.

I don't jump.

I have about a million texts and missed messages, but there's only one I care about.

hey kid. i herd. cant believe it. drop by?

It's very late when I take him up on his offer. The corridor outside his room is eerie and dark, but I hear someone singing from a nearby room, about how happiness is a state of mind. I knock softly on his door three times. I'm half hoping he's asleep by now, that he won't hear, because I need him, and I need to stop needing him, but the door swings open, and he's there, dark brown hair in his eyes, his chest—inches away—heaving. He sniffs, wipes at his face with the back of his hand. He's in his boxers.

"Noah!" he says, in a hoarse voice. "Come in. Come in. You look extravagantly awful. Great to see you. Man, you look awful."

I shut the door behind me.

He opens his arms to give me a hug—we both hesitate, because he's half naked. But then we go for it. Our bodies fit together so easily and his heart thumps against my chest. His hand brushes the top of my head gently, and I close my eyes, press my face into his neck.

Martin Singer (Friends)

Studying: **Russian Studies**

From: **Miami, Florida**

Lives in: **Lakeside Apartments (Apartment 112)**

Member of:

FLY
Westing Theater Troupe
Westing Literary Magazine

Noah Falls, Alex Grant beat your Factoryfarmville high score

Play Factoryfarmville now?

Say something to Martin . . .

Kevin Doherty

RIP, mensch. Thanks for lending me your Subaltern politics notes.

Ellen Iverson

Rest is peace, sweetie. It's a shame our plans will never go through. I'll miss you.

Robert Calahan

rot in hell you fly fucker.

He pulls away, places a hand on my shoulder. His splash-colored eyes blink. "You're crying," he says. He's breathing hard. He can't seem to catch his breath.

I reach into my pocket and withdraw a package of Skittles I got from the basement vending machines. "Please."

"God," he says, pained. He pulls on a shirt, a pair of shorts. He takes the package gently from me and places it on the table while I stand near the door like an idiot.

Why did I come here?

"I'm sorry," I say. I can't bring myself to say what I'm sorry for, so I settle on, "It's late."

He sits down on his bed, pats the spot next to him.

I sit down so our legs are touching.

"I was on the library roof," I say, as if that will clarify the matter.

"I'm sorry, Noah."

I nod. I want to tell Zach what some kids are saying. That the police shot Marty in the back. Why would they shoot him in the back? But instead, I say, "Fireworks got cancelled this year."

"I know, I *know*," he whispers.

Out in the hall someone runs past the room, their steps echoing.

Zach smiles without actually looking at me. "People here don't sleep."

I don't respond.

My cheeks are wet.

Does he notice? Of course he does.

And then he wraps his arms around me and I wrap my arms around him. We lean back together, and I bang my ear on the headboard. His shirt reads *Biology is my life*. I press my face into *Biology*.

"I'm still awkward," I mumble into the fabric.

"It didn't escape my notice," he says. "You're all bones. All scaffolding."

"He took the Polo key," I say, ignoring the drama joke. "I looked for it and it's gone. But he should've known the ladders wouldn't be there. I mean, he was with us. That's what I don't get."

Zach speaks haltingly, like he's afraid to contradict me. "It's hard to say," he says, his voice somewhere above my head.

"If Melanie hadn't—that night—he and F.L.Y. wouldn't have had to rush the main gate. He should've known. That's what I don't get."

"He stood up there a long time," Zach says.

"Everyone saying different things. That he got shot. That he escaped."

"What would you *want* to have happened?" he asks. He pulls a blanket over us, over our heads. "Now if we only had some Skittles," he adds.

I want to laugh and I want to cry.

I reach out from under the blanket, grab the packet from the table, then settle back under. It's dark and I can't see, but I find his hands, slip the package into them. I hear the tear, feel the candy spill over us. We pop them in our mouths and I listen to him chew.

"Make up a story, kid, any story you want," he says through a mouthful. "The best story you can possibly think of."

"Okay," I say. "*Okay*. What about PPV is a biological weapon that accidentally got released into the general population. Marty found out, organized a rebellion. Of course they had to make it look like they got him."

"Of course," Zach says. "Like, the electorate would *totally* hold the government responsible for wiping out American children instead of North Korean ones."

"Actually, that's the thing. It was a biological weapon designed to be used against centipedes and millipedes."

"Well, I can at least see where they were coming from with that," Zach says.

"Marty's in Hawaii now, drinking out of a coconut and generally having a great time."

"But *hey*, here's one thing you didn't answer," he says. "Why did he take the key?"

"To remember us by," I say immediately. "He knew they would've moved the ladders. It wasn't about the ladders or the shed. He just wanted *something*. The key's a metaphor, of course. But for what I don't know."

"More metaphors," Zach continues, fitting another one into my mouth. "Skittles, bear wrestling . . .

"Have you noticed," Zach says, "We only ever speak in metaphors, when we're absolutely bent on saying something meaningful? God, it's so annoying.

"Like—life is an ocean and we're in a paddleboat. Paddling," he says, and I can hear the smile in his voice.

"Because that's what paddleboats are for," I say.

"*Exactly*, kid. Or *hey*, I got another," he says. "Life is one of those balloons you get when you're six and let go of and watch get smaller and smaller—"

"Until it gets caught in a tree."

"*Exactly*."

"Life is"—I pause, thinking—"eating at the cafeteria. Once a year they serve something decent but the rest of the time all you get is the same shit over and over again."

He laughs. "Nah, I got it. Life is a mirage in a desert."

"That's so deep, Zach. It's so deep it's like a lake you can't see the bottom of."

"Are you—are you using a metaphor to rip on my metaphor?"

I shake my head. "I wouldn't do that."

If I can rip metaphorically on his metaphors, why should anything else matter? What more do you need? I want to ask him that, but I can't.

I hold him tighter, and he gasps.

"I'm sorry," I say immediately.

But his body has gone rigid.

I throw the blanket off us.

His face is white, sweaty. He is covered in Skittles.

"I get—*spasms*," he says, and closes his eyes. "I have painkillers in my closet. Top shelf."

I grab the pills, and he sits up, downs a couple with a long sip from a water bottle. He rests his head against the headboard and sighs.

The pills are contraband, which means he's in a lot of pain and he doesn't want the doctors at Wellness to know.

"I feel so *weak*," he says. His eyelids grow heavy, flutter. "How long is it, before Apep comes?"

"Eleven days," I say.

"They'll send a team up there into space to blow it apart," he says. "They have to. It's probably this top-secret mission. Like in this movie I watched . . ."

"It'll probably miss."

"They have to," he says. His eyes flutter again, then close, and just like that he's asleep. I listen to him snore and try to muster the will to go home to an apartment without Marty.

234

An Apology to Our Users

Here at AwayWeGo, we've always set the bar for customer service sky-high because we've always known that our users are so much more than customers. In partnership with Westing Academy, it has been our deepest privilege to help Westing students foster meaningful connections with one another and their families outside, and it is our deepest hope that our efforts might serve as a model for broader implementation within the National Recovery Program.

It was with these sky-high expectations that we launched our AwayWeKnow news module two years ago. This initiative was integral to our team's evolving vision of what a social network could be. If AwayWeGo has always served to promote connectivity and understanding between Westing students, it seemed only natural to extend that connectivity and understanding between students and the wider world.

Since the beginning of our AwayWeKnow initiative, however, it has always been our policy not to report on the National Recovery Program, so as not to compromise the political neutrality of the Westing experiment, and because we believed wholeheartedly in Westing's vision of giving each and every student a chance at a normal life, unbesieged by fear and worry. But in light of yesterday's tragedy, we would like to acknowledge that this lack of reporting may have contributed to a climate of apprehension and misperception and mistrust. As the only news provider for Westing students, we have a duty to educate our readers, and it is a duty we failed to uphold. For this, we owe users our deepest apologies.

Everything we do at AwayWeGo is aimed at allowing Westing students and families to navigate the National Recovery Program in the most humane way possible. As such, we are reinventing the AwayWeKnow user experience as we speak. We know users expect the world from us, and we are going to work night and day to deliver it.

Lane Cusack, CEO of AwayWeGo

THE TASTE OF NIRVANA

The news content on AwayWeGo changes overnight.

We know, finally, where it is the sick kids go.

In between articles about The Great Cliché and who was truly responsible for the Egyptian pyramids (ancient aliens?), there are stories we've never seen before.

Stories about the National Recovery Program.

Two hundred thousand children infected in the United States alone, dispersed to over a thousand recovery centers and three hundred tertiary care facilities throughout the country.

There are reports of worsening conditions in the improvised mass recovery clinics—life expectancy for youths in recovery at IMRCs is estimated at 4.7 years, two years lower than the national average.

The top daily story is a photo-essay that examines conditions in three different tertiary care facilities nationwide, one of which is located in Vermont, though the article doesn't specify where.

The conditions aren't great. The Vermont facility has six beds to a room.

"Doctors and nurses at tertiary stage facilities are widely acknowledged to be overworked and underpaid, and new data published in *JAMA Internal Medicine* found that medical error rates have risen by 15% over the past few years, as more and more youths in recovery enter tertiary care."

There is no evidence of vivisection and human science experiments. There is no evidence of our memories being downloaded onto chips and sold to their highest bidder. But then, of course, there wouldn't be.

I don't know what to believe about what to believe.

I've been eating scrambled eggs a lot.

In the kitchen, I crack an egg. A second.

There are little would-be chicks inside.

A third. A fourth.

With a fork, I turn them into yellow soup. I make them one. Next, I pour them into a hot frying pan. They spread, then stiffen. I add a little cheese. Some tomatoes.

There, little chicks. There is your afterlife. Is it everything you hoped for?

I get our plates ready—mine and Alice's—end up tripping over a bucket Alice set out to catch a leak in our ceiling. The overturned bucket sends waves across the floor. I mop the water up with a paper towel. Once that's done, I bring the plates over to the table and we dig in. Breakfast tastes like nirvana. Nirvana could've used a little more salt, though. The Buddhists never tell you that part.

"Noah, if you want to talk—"

I listen to the drip of the leak. "Sure, thanks."

"He was such a nice kid—"

Kid. God. Dr. Laura Sanberg, who discovered and named the Peter Pan Virus twenty years ago, she understood. We try to act grown-up, but it's all make-believe, pretend, like playing house when you're in kindergarten, with some bossy, ponytailed wife serving you invisible porridge in a plastic pot, porridge that tastes like air and dreams—in short, nothing at all.

Alice dips a forkful of scrambled eggs into the ketchup, brings it up to her mouth. "He would hold the door for you. Even when you were thirty feet away."

238

"You'd have to run, since you felt bad." My eyes burn. I turn so Alice can't see my face.

"He'd quote Pushkin to me."

"Tolstoy to me," I said. "But when we say Marty's nice. *Was* nice. My grammar, I still mess it up sometimes."

She scoots her seat closer to me and I can't breathe, so I push her away. "You know, for months you tried to drag me here and there, to services, to this meeting and that, wanted me to believe whatever the hell you believe. Well, I'm listening now. Convert me. Save me. Show me how to believe. Show me how to manifest my best self before—"

"You're being cruel."

"Why? Isn't this what you want?"

She bites her lip. "Do you remember Richard?" she says.

"Richard?"

"The one with the golden retriever. He *died*, Noah. He died when we were still kids. Not from PPV. In that pool of his. I don't know what happened. I think maybe he hit his head, but it was so long ago. I went to his funeral. I stopped believing in God, after that."

That takes me aback.

"You go to chapel. You dragged me to Bible study."

"I did. You trolled the whole time."

"I did not—"

"You brought spaghetti from the cafeteria and started talking about how you were eating the Flying Spaghetti Monster."

I can't help it. I laugh.

"I forgot," I admit.

"You said God goes really well with ketchup."

"You have a good memory," I say, quiet.

"The reason," she says. "The reason I go to church and Bible study—I think it's beautiful to be around people who believe in something. I don't believe in God, but I believe in people. *Noah, are you—*"

"I'm okay," I say, wiping at my eyes angrily. "I'm not—I'm sorry. It's just. It's not enough. For me. If that makes you feel better—"

"We were his friends, Noah."

"When has friends ever been enough, Alice?"

She has no answer for me.

SORRY, MARTY

It is September 22nd today.

I'm on my laptop in the kitchen, scrolling through articles. Every learned astronomer on AwayWeKnow testifies to The Great Cliché's "infinitesmal probability of terrestrial impact."

I lean my chair back, and imagine:

In the event of impact, the energy released would be equal to that of twenty thousand Hiroshimas, leveling everything within one to two hundred miles of the epicenter, sending enough dust into the atmosphere to block out the sun. If The Great Cliché landed in the ocean, tsunamis hundreds of feet high would sweep the coasts, washing away cities like New York and Tokyo and Rio De Janeiro, cities I've never been to but that have always occupied vast spaces in my mind.

I shut my laptop with a click, stuff it in my backpack. On the way to psych class, leaves crunch softly beneath my feet; my reflection follows me as I walk along the lake until I take the fork in the path that leads me past the front of Galloway, where the Believers are gathered on the lawn outside the main entrance, holding banners in support of F.L.Y.

A chill sweeps through me when I see Marty's face on the banners.

In the academic quad, teachers stream from building to building, classes and clubs continue. A group of students are hula hooping on the grass by Lombardy. There is a one in ten thousand chance that the earth will rock in its orbit, grow cold and dark, because the universe has no more intrinsic meaning than a mediocre superhero movie like *Salvation Day*, in which a villain named The Cosmic Jester attaches giant rockets to the moon and puts it on an intercept course with Earth, a tale told by an idiot, full of sound and fury, signifying nothing. In other words, it is the ideal time for hula hooping. Sometimes my gaze catches on the long blue stretches of sky, but for the most part, I just. Keep. Going.

In psych, I sit near the back. We're learning about grief and mourning. We learned that it takes six months to get over the death of a loved one. Presumably, on the first day of the seventh month, you wake up and think to yourself, "Hey, that sucker's dead, but I'm not. I'm going to take six shots of vodka now, because I can. Yes, I know it's seven-thirty a.m. Yes, with my Cheerios. What of it?"

There's a boy with tight jeans and the faint bristle of a beard beside me. I want to turn to him and say: *I am still here.* This is my constant refrain, here at Westing, maybe it's everyone's refrain the whole world over, sick or healthy, I don't know.

I want to say: We invented language for the sole purpose of issuing this reminder.

When I return to my apartment from class, there's a note pinned to the door from the office of residential life, stating Alice and I have to find a replacement for Marty, or else they'll assign someone to us. I crumple the note and throw it into the trash so Alice doesn't see it, and then I settle into the kitchen, on my computer, with every intention of playing Factoryfarmville for the next eight hours straight, to beat Connor Grant's most recent high score, because he's bumped me out of the Top Ten Hall of Fame. Maybe you can reduce friendship to playing a game—constructing a set of rules inside which you build a story together. In this case, me and Connor Grant must be bffs (sorry, Marty).

I've slaughtered a hundred twenty-seven cows and turned their hooves into McDonald's beef patties when I get a text from Jane, telling me she had another fainting spell.

orientation leader, want to come make sure i dont drop dead? :)

She's playing Zombie Survival in her bed at Wellness, grimacing and tapping maddeningly on her laptop keys as a headless zombie reaches for her.

She blows him away with a machine gun.

She glances up, then back at the screen. "I'm under observation," she says, in the same tone someone else would use to announce they've been sentenced to life without parole.

"I prefer Age of Rome," I say.

"I know," she says, rolling her eyes. "You're always on the high score list. It's a little sad."

I laugh. "What can I say? It's my legacy."

"Getting sadder," she says.

"Virtual accomplishments are still accomplishments," I insist.

"Saddest," she says, and gives me a pitying look.

"Zombies has a cooperative mode," I say.

We play Zombie Survival together, both of us craned over her screen. We move through an abandoned warehouse, mowing down one undead minion after another, and I realize Alice was right about becoming orientation leaders. Sitting here with Jane, saving the world one zombie at a time, racking up the highest score we can manage before we run out of bullets and become zombie food, that feels right, just the way calling EMS for Ally did.

In fact, mowing down zombies together feels more than right.

It makes me feel whole.

I cannot simply disappear when there are more zombies to slay.

SEPTEMBER 26TH

The last day begins as all days do: the earth spins, the sun rises, my alarm clock blares.

But I realize something as I listen to that dreaded screech, as I run through the morning chill, breath white, eyes closing, closing; as I take a hot shower; as I sit on the toilet, wrapped in two towels, completely wrapped, gazing at the porcelain tub while the water sinks down the drain; as I swallow a fork or two of mediocre scrambled eggs, breakfast of the gods; as I leaf carelessly through an assigned reading, Escobar's *Territories of Difference*, which might as well be *Territories of* In*difference*.

The one-in-ten thousand odds of Apep hitting earth are only as trustworthy as their source.

Why should I believe anything Westing lets us read, what with Marty gone?

So tonight, I will gather with all the rest of the Believers, on the lawn around Sunset Lake, for a midnight picnic, and, under Peter and Wendy's watchful gaze, I will wait for the world to end.

I need the world to end.

It will be simpler, this way, easier. No more worry and uncertainty, no more unsolved mysteries. This is my plan and it makes me so happy, to have a plan for the future, a story to fulfill. I know what I am here to do.

I feel like I'm on stage again—the one and only place where I don't have to act.

Maybe I will hold Alice's palm in my right hand and Zach's

palm in my left and we will wait for the clock to hit 11:37 p.m.

That would be the perfect end.

Except that's not what happens.

At five p.m., my pants emit a beep. I steal a glance at my phone when the teacher turns her back. The guy sitting opposite me gives me a dirty look, but I don't care. The text is from Zach.

i need help. pleaes.

I leave the lecture hall. Stop at nearby bathroom. Splash water in my face. When I get to his room, he's on the floor, on his side, bedcovers everywhere.

"Can't move," is all he says.

I pick him up, help him to his bed. He's talking, talking. "Woke up yesterday and couldn't move my legs. Can't move my legs. But I needed to make it to today. I made it to today."

Lines of sweat worm their way down his face, his arms. I've never seen him panicked before, not like this.

"Noah," he says. "They see me like this and I suppose they're going to take me away now."

"How long have you been like—*this*?"

"They're going to take me away now."

"Zach, how long have you—"

"Yesterday. I kept hoping. Kept waiting. I thought I'd wake up today and be better, good days and bad days. Sometimes my legs go numb. But not like this. I can't *move* them, Noah. And I'm losing—I can't feel the left side of my face."

I've never seen someone this bad. They're always taken away before they get this bad.

"Have you told anyone?"

"Addie would flip. She would freak. She knocked on the door but I can't deal with that. Right now. I don't know if I love her.

Isn't that crazy? After all that. I don't know what I'm saying. I'm so—God, I need you to help me."

I stand there, as paralyzed as he is.

He takes a deep breath. "I need—" He looks away. He points to his closet. "The painkillers. Top shelf."

"I remember," I say, find the bottle, and hand it to him. He fumbles with the cap, can't get it open. I look away. He laughs; there's no humor in it.

"Get it open for me, will you?"

I open it, pretending to have some difficulty.

He takes it from me. "Thanks, Noah," he says. One look inside, and his face falls. "Fuck," he says. "Fuck fuck fuck fuck fuck." He throws the bottle against the wall. I count three pills rolling on the floor. Pick up the bottle. Empty inside.

"I thought there were more. Thought there were more. Fuck," he says. "God," he says. "Shit."

His phone rings and he ignores it. I think he's crying now, but I'm not sure, since his face is already drenched from sweat.

"Three's not enough?" I ask. I'm about to reach down and try to pick the pills up.

"*Fuck*, Noah. I had an appointment at Wellness today. They keep calling. I told them I forgot and they made me reschedule for five-thirty. When I don't show up, they're going to send someone here—second they see me like this they'll—" He bites his lip and, with apparent difficulty, says, "I just wanted to know if Apep, I couldn't save anyone, I mean, Polo Club couldn't, but I thought, I don't know what I thought, but if Apep doesn't hit— they shot Marty and now they're going to take me God knows where. I don't know what I want, but I don't want that. I'm sorry, Noah."

"It's okay," I say, even though it couldn't be farther from okay.

"I'm sorry because—because I need to ask you to help me. I need you to do something. Horrible."

My eyes meet his red, watery ones.

"If Apep doesn't hit, we can't let them take me. I don't want them to take me. I wanted to save—" his voice breaks. "I know I promised we'd figure it out, but I don't want to know which stories are true and which aren't. I don't want to know where the sick kids go, okay? That's the truth, kid. I'm sorry, but I don't."

I understand now why he's called me here, why he needs me, why he was upset that the bottle only had three pills.

"No," I say. "I *can't*, Zach."

"Please—"

"I can't."

"Noah, I know. What I'm asking is horrible. I know, I know, *I know*. I'm sorry it's you. It shouldn't be you. But I have nobody else. I tried—I texted, I called, there's nobody else and Addie will freak, she won't understand, and you're always so good at responding to texts—"

"Zach, I *can't*."

"I know I said I'd do it. The one who goes away first. I said I'd be the one to do it, to tell you all what's true and what's not, but God, Noah. I'm *scared*. I don't *want* to know if it's heaven they're taking us to or a crematorium or heaven via a crematorium. I don't want them to cut into me and drug me and take notes to see what effect dosage X has and what effect candidate Y has or download my memories onto a chip. Worst of all, kid, I'll lie in some comfortable bed with fluffed pillows till I die and there will be painkillers and catheter tubes and this white room and faces I don't recognize, I won't know who I *am*—"

"We don't know that," I say, recalling a theory popular at Richmond. "There could be prototype treatments at the tertiary centers. Prototype cures. We don't know. You could get better."

He gives me an incredulous look, and I repeat, "We don't know."

"You don't really believe that, Noah. You've seen those tertiary care flyers." He adds, "Incontinence support."

I don't know what I believe. For a long time I believed in nothing and now I don't even know if I believe in that. I slump down, to the floor. Stare up at him. "Shall I beat you to death with my bare hands?"

"Thank you, Noah," he says quietly. "You're a good friend. You're one of my favorite people. Did I ever tell you that?"

"Yes," I say.

"First I want to see Apep," he says, softly. "I want to know whether we'll be saved or not. I want the government to blow it out of the sky. And then—we can figure the rest out then."

"The chances it gets anywhere near Earth are *minute*. You do realize that, don't you?"

I say it to hurt him. Because it's not fair, what he's asking me to do, to help him do.

"Or so the government would say, wouldn't they?" he retorts so fast it's like he's had the line rehearsed and ready for me.

I sigh. There's no use arguing. "I know a place with a great view."

The key is not to think, I think.

Movement. Pure movement.

Jog back to my apartment. Wheel Alice's wheelchair outside. Wheel it to Clover House. Approach Zach's door. Stop. Stop. Turn around. Ride the elevator down to the basement. Stare at the vending machine. Punch F7. Take the Skittles. Ride the elevator to the second floor. Knock.

Give Zach the Skittles. Listen to him say, "I'll save them for later."

Help Zach into the chair. Wheel him to the library. To one of the twenty-four-hour study rooms with their plush chairs and humming computers. Pretend to read Escobar's *Territories of Difference*.

Realize a response paper is due tomorrow.

Laugh out loud. A literal LOL.

Have people stare; even now, even today, people are studying.

Have Zach stare.

Find yourself unable to stop laughing.

Excuse yourself.

Go to the bathroom. Hear pant pocket beep. Ignore it. Sit in a stall. Read the graffiti on the paper towel dispenser. Someone has drawn a rather hairy pair of balls.

Remember the director's words.

There are Michelangelos here. Michelangelos and Sapphos.

Laugh out loud again.

Say, "So only Michelangelos deserve to live?"

Flush the toilet for the hell of it.

Step out of the stall and run hands through warm water. A boy looks back from inside the mirror. He is stuck.

Back in the twenty-four-hour room.

Listen to Zach say, in a whisper, "How do you think they'll do it? When they save us. They'll probably nuke it."

Not know what to tell him.

Say, "It helps to have someone like Marty write the right words out for you."

You are making no sense.

You are aware of this.

At a few minutes past eleven, when the library is mostly

deserted, bring Zach up to the top floor, to a window that leads out onto the roof. Pants beep again. Ignore them. The window is locked.

Carry a nearby chair to the window. Lift it overhead.

Bring it down, once, twice.

Listen to the tinkle of glass. Listen to an alarm go off.

Pick Zach up, out of the wheelchair.

Almost trip. Step through the window. Hit head.

Sharp, throbbing pain.

Nearly drop him. His hands around your neck. Foreheads inches apart. Lips inches apart, yours cracked and bleeding from leprosy, his perfect and smooth. The alarm, blaring.

Step, step, step.

Drop to knees a few feet away from the edge. Put him down.

Listen to the alarm.

Want to speak.

Have nothing to say.

Force yourself. "Do you want Apep to hit?"

He doesn't answer right away. Then, "I don't know. Oh kid, what do I know? You know what I want? I want the government to blow it apart. I want them to blow it out of the sky. I want them to save us all. I want a light show, fireworks. That would be a great last memory. I couldn't save anyone, but maybe they can save me."

The sound of plastic ripping. An outstretched hand. "Here," he says. He gives me three yellows in a row.

I eat them, and say, "I hate yellows."

"I know. You scrunch up your face. It was always a mystery to me, Noah, why you were so fond of me."

Knots in my throat, my chest.

"I'm not," I say. "I'm just really good at answering texts."

"Ouch," he says. "I suppose I deserve it. God, I suppose I deserve worse." He glances over the edge of the roof.

"Why did you give me a yellow if you knew I hated yellows?"

"I don't know," he says with a weary sigh, and it feels like he's accepted something. "I think you've always wanted something from me I couldn't give, kid. I think you've always thought I was someone I wasn't."

"I think you're the best," I say. "You helped me with my room, and you showed me that squirrel because you felt bad. We raced in the rain. You gave me your shirt. You started Polo and you were there for Melanie and you're always so kind. I like everything about you."

I want to tell him about how he brushed his finger through my hair, that small, intimate gesture. A friend does not brush a friend's hair.

"God," he says.

"So why do you always have to do things like—give me the yellows?"

"The world's about to be blown apart and all you can think about—"

"It wasn't just me," I say. "Was it?"

Because it matters more than ever if what I felt was real, if what I felt was returned, especially if the world is about to be blown apart. If all this time I've been living in a fantasy, then I might as well just off and vanish.

"Check the time," he says, scanning the night above.

The alarm's still blaring.

"I know you felt something," I say.

"Check the time, Noah."

I do.

There is a minute and a half left.

I tell him so.

There is a minute left.

I tell him so.

There are forty-five seconds left.

I tell him so.

Our eyes are set on the sky, and the stars in the sky, Peter and Wendy and beyond them the stars we'll never see, even in the night, as we wait for the great tragic powers of the world to reveal themselves.

There are twenty seconds.

"You're not going to respond?"

There are ten seconds.

I put a hand on his shoulder. "Why won't you tell me?"

He brushes my hand off, looks at me sadly. "I don't want to ruin our end of the world. Can't you see that?"

There are five seconds.

And four.

And three.

And two.

And one.

We wait.

We wait.

We wait.

"Maybe they were wrong," I say eventually.

And then we see it.

A red streak in the sky.

"They're going to do it," Zach says, watching, his mouth hanging open. We wait to be saved, for that red streak to burst into a thousand smaller ones.

It doesn't happen.

The red streak passes us by, like all those learned astronomers said it would, like AwayWeKnow said it would. A minute elapses, and another, and I am in pain, because the world is still here, and I am still here, because there are no easy solutions, no deus ex machinas, no great rescues, because the world doesn't end with a bang but with a whimper, because you have to live with that thin, papery feeling no matter how much you want to rage, rage against the dying of the light.

"Well," Zach says, and pitches forward, toward the edge, but I grab his arm.

"We were together," I plead.

"God, kid, let me go," he says, dragging me till we're both about to topple over. He is surprisingly strong. "I didn't want to hurt you, that's why I never told you, but it felt wrong. I'm not that way. Can't you understand that? Can't you?"

Security carts rev in the distance above the sound of the alarm.

His hands are on my chest, pushing.

"You brushed your hands through my hair."

"I can't be whoever you want me to be."

"We metaphorically made fun of each other's metaphors."

"What are you even *talking* about?" he asks. He's crying.

"We played ring-around-the-rosie."

"I barely remember," he says. "It was so late."

And if he doesn't remember, how do I know I didn't make it up? How do I know what is true and what is not? If I am my memories, and my memories are fictions, fabrications, then what am I?

"I'm not crying," I say, ridiculously, as I've been at it since I broke the window.

"That day in the woods, I hated that I couldn't imagine you

ever hurting anyone. I knew you'd never escape. I knew you'd sit behind these walls till you rot."

"Why are you saying this?"

"Because I'm a terrible person," he says. "Because I'm using you. I couldn't have dragged myself here without you. Don't you see that?"

I let go of him, put my hands to my ears, even though it's useless, even though I can't unhear what he's already said. "Do you think it'll be easier if I hate you?"

I don't know if it's what I said, or how pathetic I must look, but something in him breaks. He covers my hands in his and that simple gesture makes me believe again, in everything that he's just told me is untrue.

"I'm not saying that's what I was doing," he says, in a low voice. "But I think that would make things easier. Wouldn't it?"

I let my hands fall to my sides.

"You're the only person who's ever—" he starts, but he can't say it. "I don't think Addie ever loved me." He shakes his head. "God, did I ever think this was going to go so differently."

I can see, now, he's going to do it. The resolve in his eyes.

"I'm sorry if I hurt you," he says. "You're my best friend, for doing this. I'm sorry I couldn't make us both happy."

He leans back, lifts his arms up, over his head, and falls.

The edge is right there, so close. I stand where Zach sat a moment before, my arms outstretched, eyes closed. My heart hammers so hard I can feel it in my ears.

The Great Cliché hurtles somewhere above.

It was never going to hit the earth.

Zach is splayed on the ground below, surrounded by a spray of Skittles.

We were never going to be together.

But that, more than anything, was the story I believed in. We have so many stories to choose from at Westing. The Great Cliché, the Home Hotline, the possibility of escaping over the walls. Westing's nefarious collaboration with aliens. Mad scientists who download our memories onto chips to sell to the highest bidder. Marty the hero, who discovers PPV is really a biological weapon against centipedes and escapes to Mexico to tan it up. The end of the world! All these stories, because the alternative is too hard to take seriously: incontinence support; giving Michelangelos and Sapphos castles and shit while Alex reads books beside a urinal; we are weak and small before the great tragic powers of the world, and so are our parents, and so are our friends; we will never know why some kids get sick and some kids do not; we will never know where away we go.

With Zach gone, I am almost nothing. A strong wind will blow me away. But there's only one thing I still believe in, one story I have left inside me, and that's Neverland.

I laugh, then, standing on the roof with my arms outstretched, because Polo Club had it all wrong. Marty, the one person who should've had it right, got it all wrong.

We should've never fixed upon those ladders, upon scaling the walls.

That would never get us where we wanted to go.

No, the answer was right next to the ladders.

I even hit my foot on it.

I take out my phone to make a few calls, because Polo Club's not finished yet.

The more I move, the less time I have to feel. Even so, watching the boy you love kill himself really takes it out of you. A peek around the corner of the greenhouse gives me a clear view of the construction shed, and the guards stationed by its door.

"Yo, how many, bro?" Nigel whispers into my ear as I retreat into cover. I can smell the alcohol on his breath. Zach fell in a rain of Skittles—what am I supposed to feel? I don't know. I don't know I don't know I don't know.

"Noah?" Nigel repeats.

"Two," I force myself to say. "But we need the key first. You *sure* the old man has a spare?"

"Old coot has, like, seven spares," Nigel assures me.

We use the light from our phones to guide us through the dark until we find the window to the groundskeeper's office. I try to force it up, but it's locked, so I take my shirt off and Nigel whistles approvingly as I wrap it around my hand like a glove.

"Can you not act like a five-year-old for five seconds?" Melanie hisses.

"She has a point, Nigey," Grace says.

"Yo, I'm a red-blooded human being," Nigel says. "I'm admiring the way the moonlight plays off his nips."

I haven't told them about Zach, yet. I don't know if I can.

I concentrate on action: for the second time that night, I break a window. I climb through, doing my best to avoid cutting myself on the jagged edges of glass. I succeed, only to land awkwardly and twist my ankle.

"Fuck," I say, groping blindly for the light switch along the wall. I touch something smooth, and it crashes. I nearly trip over it.

"Noah!" Grace calls. "You alive in there?"

"Alive and pretty," I call back.

How can I be doing this now? How can I how can I how can

I? How can I joke? How are jokes possible in a world so full of tragic powers?

My eyes adjust and there's the old man's coffeemaker lying broken on the floor.

Thuds from behind, as the rest of Polo Club, or what remains of us, follows me inside. There is the sound of their footsteps scraping the ground, but all I can think about is the coffeemaker, *Cuisinart* or *Mr. Coffee* or whatever, and how the old man's daughter bought it for him. Why did I have to go and break it?

I find the light switch and hit it. The keys hang on the far wall. Of course I have no idea which is which.

We all turn to Nigel expectantly, as before.

"I thought I was the five-year-old," he says reproachfully.

Grace nudges him with her elbow.

"Which one is it already?" Melanie asks. "I don't want to be here all night."

Nigel squints. "I'm, uh, not sure." He grabs one, seemingly at random, tosses it to me. "I think that's it."

"You *think*," Melanie says.

"He's doing his best," Grace says. "Don't pressure him."

They're already moving toward the window, Nigel's out first, cursing all the while, I think he cut his hand, then Melanie, and as for me, I'm searching for paper and a pen, because I can't leave, not like this, with the coffeemaker broken.

"Noah," Grace says, with concern. She's paused by the window, one foot on the sill, about to climb out. "What are you doing?"

"I don't know," I say.

But I do.

I set the broken coffeemaker back on the desk, and on a piece of paper I write a minor apology in the light from the window. Then I'm out again, my feet hitting the ground, pain shooting through my leg. I peek around the corner of the greenhouse. The guards are exactly as before, sitting on two foldout plastic chairs by the construction shed. One leans over, and lights the other's cigarette.

"I have an idea," Melanie says. She motions to Grace and Nigel. "We'll distract them. We'll say some jackasses broke into the groundskeeper's office, lead them around the other side."

I wish I could tell the three of them what this means to me. They understand and they also don't. I don't know how to explain. They will have to see. They will have to feel it. I should tell them about Zach now, at least, but I don't, I can't, I need to keep him to myself for a little while longer; I need something to hold inside.

"Thank you," I say.

Nigel's hand is shaking mine. "Good luck, sexy-licious."

Then Grace looms over me. I wince from the strength of her grip. "Run fast, Noah."

Then Melanie, who stares skeptically at my hand and reminds me, "I don't subscribe to social conventions that—oh what the fuck." And she gives me a hug.

"Okay," I say. To all three, "Remember to look up."

And then they're running to meet the guards, Melanie's yelling about teenage vandalism, the lack of respect for private property, the three of them gesticulating. They lead the guards around the opposite side of the greenhouse, and I laugh because *it works*, I'm half limping, half running now, as fast as I can, the door of the shed growing larger, the key in my hand, I'm ignoring the pain in my leg, fitting the key in the lock with trembling hands, but it won't work, *of course*, and I laugh again, of course it won't work, but there's not much time, the guards will realize something's up soon, so I take a few steps back, and I ram the door with my shoulder. It shakes but doesn't give way. I ram it again, and this time it buckles a bit, but holds. It takes three more tries until it bursts open, and the ladders, the ladders are no longer here, of course they moved them, but I'm not looking for the ladders, I'm looking for the fireworks we saw that day that feels so long ago, I'm grabbing a box of the fireworks, and running, my leg feels likely to fall off and so does my bruised arm, but I'm running, toward the lake, down the cobblestone paths that are worn into my muscle memory, that I could run with my eyes closed, I have this whole campus imprinted into me, and once I'm at the lake I dart through throngs of students still waiting for an end of the world that's not going to come, and then I'm racing up Sunset Hill, my arms heavy, my arms heavier than heavy, my whole body screaming in protest, the pain in my leg sharper now, I can't drop him, I can't let him go, why does he want me to let him go, the crest is near, there are no great battles, there is only this, there are only small moments that we narrate into meaning, I can do something worthy of meaning, I can share my meaning with hundreds of others, and it can become their meaning, maybe the fact that there is no one story is what makes it possible to have individual stories, and to share them with others, and by sharing create a mythology together, a religion together, a constellation of meaning, we can escape together, this is how we defy the great tragic emptiness of the world, how we make the world full, how we become real, and then I'm standing at the top of the hill, Peter and Wendy bright above me, I have a lighter in my hands, I'm setting the fireworks off, one after another, they drift up and explode between Peter and Wendy like Skittles in the sky, and I know security is coming, I know they will stop me in a matter of seconds, but before they do, there is this perfect hush, because it is 2:33 a.m., and for this one moment, away we go to Neverland, all of Westing, all of us, all the sickly children of the world saved beneath a common blanket.

"To die," I say, "will be an awfully big adventure."